WYVERNHAIL

Also by Amelia Atwater-Rhodes

WYVERNHAIL

Amelia Atwater-Rhodes

Delacorte Press

Published by Delacorte Press
an imprint of Random House Children's Books
a division of Random House, Inc.
New York

Delacorte Press and colophon are registered trademarks of
Random House, Inc.

www.randomhouse.com/teens

Educators and librarians, for a variety of teaching tools, visit us at
www.randomhouse.com/teachers

Library of Congress Cataloging-in-Publication Data
Atwater-Rhodes, Amelia.
Wyvernhail / Amelia Atwater-Rhodes. — 1st. ed.
p. cm. — (The Kiesha'ra ; v. 5)
Summary: In order to protect the people and the world she loves from the
future she sees in increasingly horrific visions, Hai is forced to throw away
her own happiness and ascend the serpiente throne.
ISBN: 978-0-385-73436-3 (hardcover)
ISBN: 978-0-385-90442-1 (Gibraltar lib. bdg.)
[1. Fantasy.] I. Title.
PZ7.A8925Wyv 2007
[Fic]—dc22
2006101424

The text of this book is set in 12-point Loire.

Printed in the United States of America

10 9 8 7 6 5 4 3 2 1

First Edition

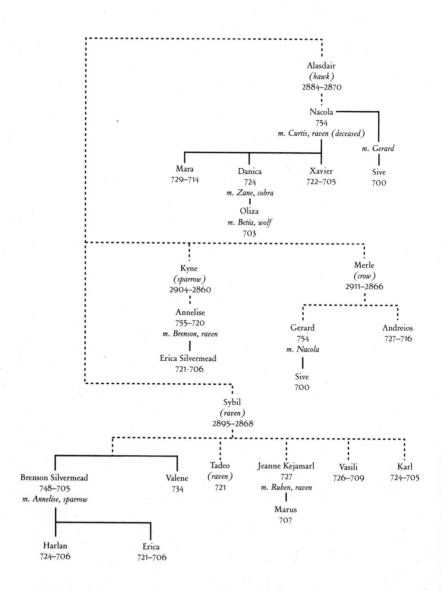

Dashed lines indicate not only a lapse of several generations, but also an indirect relation.

SHIFTERS

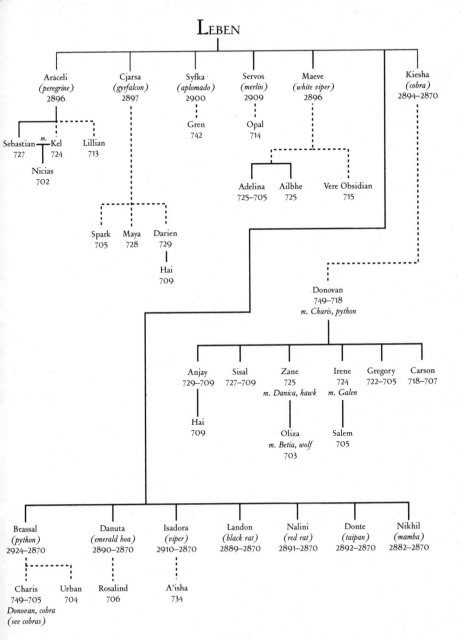

LEBEN

Aràceli
(peregrine)
2896

Cjarsa
(gyrfalcon)
2897

Syfka
(aplomado)
2900

Servos
(merlin)
2909

Maeve
(white viper)
2896

Kiesha
(cobra)
2894–2870

Sebastian — *m.* — Kel
727   724

Lillian
713

Nicias
702

Gren
742

Opal
714

Spark
705

Maya
728

Darien
729

Hai
709

Adelina
725–705

Ailbhe
725

Vere Obsidian
715

Donovan
749–718
m. Charis, python

Anjay
729–709

Sisal
727–709

Zane
725
m. Danica, hawk

Irene
724
m. Galen

Gregory
722–705

Carson
718–707

Hai
709

Oliza
m. Betia, wolf
703

Salem
705

Brassal
(python)
2924–2870

Danuta
(emerald boa)
2890–2870

Isadora
(viper)
2910–2870

Landon
(black rat)
2889–2870

Nalini
(red rat)
2891–2870

Donte
(taipan)
2892–2870

Nikhil
(mamba)
2882–2870

Charis
749–705
Donovan, cobra
(see cobras)

Urban
704

Rosalind
706

A'isha
734

WYVERNHAIL

PROLOGUE

Who am I? Lately I have wondered this, as I've struggled to discover my place in the world in which I find myself.

Mongrel, exile, stranger. I have always been tolerated, wherever I've been, but I have never been welcomed except by Ecl, the void darkness. And what does that mean, to be wanted by Nothing?

My father was Anjay Cobriana, a serpiente prince, the heir to the cobra throne. He was loved by his people and his family. Though it has been twenty-five years since Anjay's death at the hands of the hawk prince Xavier Shardae, my father's followers still say his name with reverence. They look to me, as his only child, with respect, even though I never knew him; my father was killed within days of my conception.

My mother was the falcon la'Darien'jaes'oisna'ona'saniet. Darien was young, and she was powerful. She swore her service to the Empress Cjarsa when she was still a child. Years later, she conceived me during Anjay's visit to our falcon land. The trauma of his death triggered in her a vision of events the Empress had long before struggled to hide: the creation of the ancient avian-serpiente war.

Darien stayed quiet for the months before my birth, but once I was no longer dependent on her mothering body, she began her treason, which culminated in an attempt to kill the Empress's heir, the Lady Araceli.

That was the last time my "mother" bothered to care for her child.

I was raised a mongrel in the beautiful white land of Ahnmik; I was a flaw in the center of an otherwise priceless diamond. The Empress herself took a hand in my upbringing. She alone showed me tenderness during my childhood.

My earliest memory is of my Empress holding me after my magic overwhelmed me and filled my mind with images no child should ever see. My memory is of pain and blood—and of my Empress's gentle arms and the sadness in her eyes when I burned my voice away with my screams.

After that day, Cjarsa allowed me to grow the wings of my Demi form, so that I could take to the sky. She taught me to dance, and for a few brief years I was a child. I ran with the dreams of others, laughing with the spirits of the past and the future that always walk the roads of the white city, invisible to most—but never to me. I made friends with those who did not exist, with those who might never exist, and with those who had died millennia before. I remember one woman, who most frequently filled my constant waking dreams. Though born of mixed blood, she had learned to control her power. I wanted so badly to know her—to be her—but like all my ghosts, she never looked at me.

Sometimes, when I danced, I could feel my Empress watching. She was one of the very few people who were fully real to me. When she smiled, I felt Ahnmik's magic shimmer with pleasure as if I had been granted a gift by the divine.

Then came the day when—

Ahnmik' falmay'la. *Ahnmik, help me; grant me your black peace. Do not make me think of that day.*

I can speak for ages about the lives, the hopes and fears, of others; please, keep me from my own nightmares.

I can speak of the Dasi, the ancient coven from which the falcons and the serpiente both come. I can almost feel the hot sand of the Egyptian desert beneath my feet and smell the Nile. I can see their altars. I can see them dance and pray.

I was lost in the darkness of Ecl for so long, and I was content there, until a guard sworn to my father's line—a guard with royal falcon blood I could not ignore—called to me. Duty compelled Nicias to try to pull me from my void, but it is hard to say exactly what compelled me to return.

And now here I am, a mongrel in a land of mongrels and yet still an outsider. All I have from my mother is a broken falcon form I cannot call upon, and all I have from my father is cursed blood and a black onyx signet ring to symbolize the family that I've no desire for.

She'ka'hena.

We are not.

O'she'ka'hena-a'she'ka'hena.

We never were; we never shall be. We return to the void we never left, for Mehay *is the center of all, and all is the center of nothing.*

em'Ecl'la'Hai

CHAPTER 1

Fire.

Serpiente who held to the old myths believed that the world began in fire. Out of the numb void came passion and heat, and Will too strong to be denied. Order and chaos—Ahnmik and Anhamirak—began their eternal dance, and from the embers of their battle, the world was born.

So perhaps it was not surprising that the world would end of that same heat.

I was pulled from my musings as the door opened, drawing my attention to the small two-room building in which I had been sitting cross-legged before the hearth, perhaps for several hours. I looked up as a trio of falcons entered the candle shop, their steps uncharacteristically light and their expressions unguarded.

"*Hanlah'ni-aona'pata'rrasatoth-rakuvra'pata'Diente.*" Cobras change kings, Spark observed with some amusement, as easily as the white Lady's heir changes lovers.

The four falcons who frequented this shop at the edge of the avian hills of Wyvern's Court were in hiding, criminals who would probably be executed if they ever showed themselves in the white city again. Though Spark, Maya, Opal and Gren disguised themselves as simple avian merchants in the public areas of Wyvern's Court, here they switched back to the falcon language *ha'Dasi*.

I enjoyed hearing the language of my home, even spoken by these exiles. Some of the serpents of Wyvern's Court tried to use it, but *ha'Dasi* always sounded stunted and twisted to me when it came from the tongue of a snake.

Opal emerged from the back room, his eyes heavy lidded from sleep. Without sparing a glance at me, he asked, *"Hehj' hena?"* What happened?

Gren, the owner of the candle shop, answered in the same language. "Oliza Shardae Cobriana," he announced, "has just abdicated the throne of Wyvern's Court. She and some wolf have run off in the woods together, leaving Salem and Sive holding the bag."

The words stole my breath, not because they shocked me but because they left me with a powerful sense of déjà vu. Months before, I had seen a vision of the wyvern princess dethroned. The image had been unclear, and all I had been able to do was go to Oliza and warn her: "You are about to do something that changes everything." I had hoped to make her think through her actions.

Instead, I had triggered the very events I had sought to avoid.

Around me, the falcons continued their conversation. "Changing leaders like autumn leaves is better than letting one rule for a thousand years," Gren observed.

"It makes you wonder, though, how easy it might be to put someone on the serpiente throne who would turn this land in a more favorable direction." Maya looked pointedly at me.

This was not a new argument, and Opal dismissed it before I even needed to reply. "Makes *you* wonder, perhaps," he scoffed. "One would think that several days of punishment by the Empress's Mercy would have taught you not to speak treason with every word."

"The Heir gave me to her Mercy for conceiving a *child*," Maya spat. This was the crime that had led her to flee from the falcon island. "If that is treason—"

"Which it is," Opal said, interrupting, "seeing as the Empress forbids *kajaes* from breeding."

Kajaes were falcons born without magic, freaks in a city whose inhabitants breathed power and worked spells as if they were weaving baskets. But Ahnmik's magic was poison to new life; the royal house had had only one child in the past thousand years: Araceli's son, Sebastian. *Kajaes* children were conceived more easily.

Almost as easily as *quemak*, mongrels like Opal—whose father was human, leaving Opal with the stigma of mixed blood in addition to no magic—and of course me.

"If that is treason," Maya said softly, "and is deserving of what I suffered for it, then do you think I fear a cobra's punishment? Besides, I speak only of replacing one cobra with another. It's nothing new for serpents."

Sometimes I envied Maya for the fire of her hatred. Though *kajaes*, and therefore powerless to make any change, she maintained an incredible passion that I was no longer able to feel, no matter how I tried.

7

"Sebastian's child guards the new serpiente king," Opal pointed out. "Nicias sees us all for what we are, and don't think he doesn't watch us carefully. You don't think he would stop you if you tried to—"

Maya uttered a curse. "Then we get rid of him—"

"At which point you consign to the Ecl the false queen you wish to place on the throne," I said softly, interjecting. This argument was old, and I was bored of it. "But not until I teach you agony the Mercy never dreamed of."

Silence crashed down. Unlike these four, I was not harmless *kajaes*. I had the full ability to carry out my threat, if I chose.

"Salem Cobriana is beloved by his people," I said. "The dancers adore him, because he is the first in more than eight hundred years to be raised in the nest nursery. He follows their most ancient traditions and knows them all as well as any dancer. He is supported by the previous Diente, by the beloved princess Oliza, and by the avian Tuuli Thea. Most serpents tolerate me, but only because I do nothing that offends them . . . that they know of," I added. If they knew I spent my free hours with falcons and the white vipers of the outlaw Obsidian guild, they would tolerate me far less. "Sive Shardae, on the other hand, can barely stand to be in the room with me—"

"Who cares what the hawk thinks?" Maya asked, challenging me.

"Everyone who does not wish to return to war," Gren answered for me.

I nodded. "And as you mentioned, Salem will now be guarded by Nicias Silvermead. I will kill any who touch the falcon prince. That is, if they aren't first killed by either the Wyverns or the serpiente palace guard."

Maya tossed her head. "You are forgetting that you are the rightful heir to the serpiente throne. You are Anjay Cobriana's only daughter—"

"And Salem is his nephew," I said. "*You* are forgetting two very important things. First of all, the serpiente would rebel and dethrone any who dared challenge their beloved king. No matter what my *birthright,* they would never allow me to take the throne from the one they want there."

Again Maya argued. "There are traditionalists among the serpiente who think you should be queen. I have heard them speaking. Whether or not they approve of you specifically, they think that Anjay's daughter—not the son of his younger sister—should take the throne. You are the oldest and the first in line. Blood may not matter to a serpent as much as it does to a falcon, but a cobra's blood still matters."

"The second and most important thing you are forgetting," I said, ignoring the valid but irrelevant argument, "is that I have no desire to be queen. *Breathing* is a bother to me. Why would I wish to rule?"

"*Think what you could accomplish,*" Maya said, impassioned. "Imagine a world where the serpiente followed you. Imagine if you could rally your Nicias to our cause, or—"

"I could, what, topple the white towers?" I asked. "Survive, Maya. That is all you and I can do. And for some of us, survival takes enough effort. Let it be."

"If nothing else," Maya said, "you would be able to protect those of us who are here. We would be able to live our lives without constantly fearing that the serpiente will discover us and send us away, or that the Empress will remember us and have us dragged back to the island to be put down like feral dogs. If you would not or could not fight Ahnmik on the island, you could fight the Mercy if they came for us here. The serpiente army would be able to win if you showed them how to fight a falcon. We're all *kajaes*. Our children would have no magic. They would be no threat to this realm. As Diente, you could give us a chance to have normal lives."

Tears glistened in Maya's eyes, no doubt as she remembered the infant the Mercy had ripped from her the moment it was weaned of its mother's milk.

Had my own mother ever cried this way? I thought not. Darien of Ahnmik had shown more compassion to these *kajaes*, whom she had smuggled off the island beneath the veil of her own magic, than she ever had to me, her own misbegotten child.

"Go to Salem, while he is holding his first child in his arms and feeling how precious it is," I said to Maya. "Or go to the Tuuli Thea Sive, when she is first a mother. Tell that monarch your story, and speak your plea."

"Trust a hawk?" Maya replied incredulously. "Or a cobra? What would stop them from turning me in?"

"Honor?" I suggested.

"Cobras have no honor."

I couldn't help smiling a little, though most wouldn't at that thought. "I am a cobra," I answered Maya. "*Quemak*, remember? And the other half of my blood comes from one of the Empress's Mercy. Not a good lineage for a woman you would like to place in power."

"You're a gyrfalcon," Gren argued. "And your mother isn't just one of the Mercy; she is Darien, to whom we all owe our lives—"

"Darien," I said, "who tortured your mother, Opal, for her dalliance with a human. Darien, who—"

"People change. They learn," Opal asserted. "Darien most of all. She wants to—"

"My mother *wants* a lot of things," I said. "She speaks about a great many dreams as she stands in the white city, by the right hand of the Empress, while we rot in this mongrel land."

I tried to turn away, but Maya gripped my hand.

"Hai, please, try to imagine—"

" 'Try to imagine' a world where she cares," Opal spat. "Imagine a world where our mongrel cobra has the courage and conviction of her mother. But the Empress long ago wrote that a *quemak* child will have cowardice and treason in her blood—"

"The Empress says a lot of things about *quemak,* things that may serve her agenda more than the absolute truth," Maya snapped. I tried to pull away, and she held more tightly. "Hai, listen to me! Imagine a world where a mixed-blood falcon like you isn't automatically branded a dangerous traitor. Imagine being able to study your magic, take your wings, and dance—"

I tore away from her, aware that my garnet eyes were flashing with rare temper. "I had that," I said. "And it wasn't something my mother gave to me. My *Empress* raised me, when the woman you praise was otherwise occupied. When my first *sakkri* made me scream until I lost my voice for days, Cjarsa bent her own laws and let me grow my wings and dance so I could focus my magic on the present and perhaps not see such horrors again. What did that leniency get us? I lost control, lost my wings and endangered the woman who had raised me, all because my *quemak* arrogance convinced me that I could be more than my cobra father's mistake."

"You *are*—"

"And now here I sit," I continued, "in a room full of criminals, listening to treason. So tell me, Maya, how was Cjarsa incorrect?"

Bitterly, Maya said, "You speak very highly of *your* Empress, yet you are the only one of us who is willingly here in Wyvern's Court. If you love the city so much, why don't you go back to it?"

"Give it a rest," Opal said, placing a hand on Maya's shoulder as I turned to leave. "Sometimes the Empress *is* right. *People* change. *Snakes* don't."

I did not slam the door as I left. There was no need. We had had many arguments about this here—and we would have more.

It was true that I would be allowed to return to Ahnmik if I chose. Empress Cjarsa might send someone to carry me, since I did not have wings of my own anymore. Then I would once again be able to walk in a land where the walls glistened with magic and the roads sang a melody no voice could reproduce. I could live out the rest of my days in a land where even the prison of the mad—the Halls of *shm'Ecl*, where I had spent many years—was so beautiful to behold, it could bring tears to a mortal's eyes.

So, too, could a cuckoo be raised by robins. I loved the white city, but in it, I would be that cuckoo, put into the nest by a mother more interested in using me as a political excuse than in nurturing me. If I returned, I would be Darien's pawn to use against my Empress, and that I could not stand.

CHAPTER 2

I was not the only citizen of Ahnmik who had chosen this exile. Nicias Silvermead was the acknowledged heir of Lady Araceli, who was heir to none other than the Empress herself. Yet the beautiful royal peregrine had chosen to stay in Wyvern's Court to serve the now abdicated wyvern princess, Oliza.

My loyalty to the Empress Cjarsa kept me from the white island, but my connection to Nicias kept me in Wyvern's Court—and indeed, in this reality.

I had languished in my silent madness for years before Nicias found me hiding from the pain of a shattered body and ruined dreams. His vows to the Cobriana line and royal falcon blood helped him pull me from that void, and for that salvation, I both loved Nicias and hated him. Ahnmik's reluctant prince had given me the world . . . or as much of it as I could hold. Visions of Ahnmik, shards of Wyvern's Court, fragments of pasts and futures other than my own.

I still felt trapped within Ecl's numbing ice, able to watch others live but not quite able to feel that life—except sometimes when I beheld Nicias's love for this land and its people. His passion for Wyvern's Court drove me now from Gren's candle shop to the marketplace, to see what would happen next.

Before I had even descended the northern hills, I could hear shouting.

I took another step forward, and suddenly the noise was replaced by absolute silence. I looked over the market that had just been filled with anxious, frightened and angry avians and serpents, and saw nothing but mist and the pale shimmer of falcon magic.

I squeezed my eyes closed, trying to clear the vision from my mind before it could overwhelm me. This time I succeeded in chasing away the *sakkri*, and I was grateful for that. Too often I became lost in other times and places, especially when I walked through the center of Wyvern's Court. Anhamirak's magic swirled so thickly there among the avians and the serpiente, it frequently robbed me of any scraps of control I might have had.

The shouting returned, and I entered the market.

Salem Cobriana and Sive Shardae were at the heart of the chaos. Salem, Oliza's only full-blood serpiente cousin, had stepped down off a nearby dais and was talking intently with the serpents, who had all but mobbed him. Sive, Oliza's young avian aunt, was struggling to keep some space to herself, but it was a losing battle, one that was obviously making her alistair, Prentice, very nervous. Oliza's parents, Zane and Danica, the current Diente and Tuuli Thea, both looked pale and tired, but they were trying to deal with the shocked crowd.

Oliza herself did not seem to be present.

Nicias, however, was nearby. He was moving from group to group, sometimes speaking to other guards or breaking up fights, but most often trying to hold the crowd back so they wouldn't completely overwhelm the royal family. Though I would have liked to go to him, I knew better than to attempt to distract him while he was working. I could more easily have swallowed the sea.

Instead, I waylaid a serpiente I knew, a flautist named Salokin. "What is going on?"

The red mamba quickly confirmed what the falcons had told me: "Oliza has announced her abdication." His voice was breathy and dazed, and his gaze was unfocused. "She stood on that dais and . . ." For the first time, he looked at me, as he said, "You weren't there. The Diente and the Tuuli Thea and Nacola Shardae and Salem and Sive and Prentice were all there."

"Apparently I don't merit an invitation to royal functions," I said without much shock. As Maya had said, my having cobra blood mattered to the serpiente. It did not, however, matter enough to make me family.

"But she *abdicated*. She must have spoken to you about it."

"Why would she have?" I asked. I had meddled too much in this drama already, helping Oliza spin a *sakkri* of her own after mine had foretold her abandonment of the throne. I had not been able to see that second vision, but I imagined that it was what had led to Oliza's abdication.

Which one was it? I wondered. I had seen many futures for Wyvern's Court, most of them ending with fire, as Anhamirak's magic burned out of control, or with ice, as the falcons wielded Ahnmik's power and tried to salvage what they could from the wreckage.

Salokin's eyes widened. "Why would she . . . She *abdicated*."

"So you've said, a few times now."

"The serpiente Arami just stepped down from the throne," he said, as if rewording might make the facts different.

So did the avian heir to the Tuuli Thea, I was about to say, before I realized what was troubling the mamba. "Salem will rule the serpiente well," I assured him.

"Salem is . . . very much a dancer." The words, though formed like a compliment, did not sound like one. "He was not raised to be king. He wasn't even in line to inherit. How could the Arami abdicate and not even *inform* the woman who, if not for falcon treachery, would have been heir in the first place?"

Falcon treachery. Is that how they're explaining my history these days? My father had never even known I had been conceived. Even if Anjay Cobriana had not been killed within hours of his return to serpiente land, he would not have been informed of my existence. Had Nicias not spied me in the Halls of *shm'Ecl,* Wyvern's Court would have been ignorant still.

Some, I supposed, would consider that treachery. After all, according to serpent laws, I should have been my father's heir.

"I would have to be more than half cobra to be heir to the serpiente throne," I pointed out. "Certainly I would have to be less than half falcon, since most serpents still hate and fear my mother's kind."

"Oliza was only half cobra herself," Salokin said, "and

she was beloved as Arami, despite the fact that we warred with the avians, *her* mother's people, much more recently than we did with the falcons."

I smiled slightly, somewhat amused. "Fine, perhaps it was . . . rude," I allowed, "but though Oliza and I are cousins, we aren't close. I imagine she had larger things on her mind than the guest list when she planned her abdication."

"Maybe."

My gaze drifted back toward the crowd, to where Salem had regained the dais. The cobra reached down to pull a lovely auburn-haired dancer up with him.

At first, the dancer's face seemed to be streaked with tears. She was dressed in a gown of dark plum, the serpiente color of mourning, and her skin was pale and blotched from weeping.

Then the brief vision faded, and she was vibrant and beautiful once more.

"Rosalind," Salokin said when he saw what my attention had turned to. "I imagine she is the one Salem will name serpiente queen." He shook his head.

"He will be a fine king," I said. The words were mostly empty comfort; what did I know of kings? "It isn't as if he will be without guidance. The Diente and the Naga are both still alive."

"I suppose."

"Hai!" The anxious voice that cut through our conversation belonged to Sive. The hawk had somehow struggled away from the near mob around the dais and now came to my side, perhaps out of courtesy or perhaps to take advantage of the space that most serpents gave me, wary of the "black magic" falcons could wield.

Sive would become the next avian queen, and though

she was young still, she was too old to be called a child. Her alistair, Prentice, hovered beside her, as protective as a mother hen.

"Hai, how are you?" she asked me. She reached out and took my hand in greeting, betraying her frequent contact with the serpents.

For a moment I could not answer, because at Sive's touch I saw her, several years older, glowing with joy as she held her infant in her arms. The beloved queen presented her child to her people and said her name: Aleya. She handed the babe to her alistair, and as their hands touched, I could feel the love that stretched between them.

In contrast to the earlier visions I had had, of Wyvern's Court after its destruction and of Rosalind's tears, this one was comforting.

"I . . . You will be a beautiful queen," I said, still half within the vision. "Aleya . . . the name means 'given to us.' "

Sive recoiled from me, breaking the trance.

"Th-thank you," she said, but I could see the fear in her eyes.

I was glad she stopped me, because I knew what I would have said next: *You are very much in love, but there is sorrow in your heart, too. You remember the man who was your alistair when you were a child. He often frustrated you, but you loved him despite his awkwardness.*

Prentice . . . gone, to where?

Right then he came forward, guarding his pair bond from whatever threat he felt I projected.

I started to reach out for the rest of the vision and barely managed to resist. Sive could rule peacefully with or without this man. I did not need to know when or how they would separate.

I shook my head, backing away.

"Excuse me," I said.

"Are you all right?" Salokin put a hand on my arm, and that was enough to trigger another vision of Wyvern's Court, this time in flames.

I shuddered, pulling back mentally and physically, trying to fight the *sakkri*. There was too much going on in the market. In the language of Ahnmik, Oliza's abdication would be referred to as a *sheni'le*, a decision that drastically altered the path of Fate. I had foolishly come here to see the present for myself but was on the verge of being swamped by futures.

I turned abruptly, not bothering to beg leave of the heir to the Tuuli Thea or explain myself to the flautist. I needed to be somewhere quiet.

If only I had not lost my falcon form long before, I could have grown my wings. Within minutes, I could have been beyond the bounds of Wyvern's Court, beyond the influence of Anhamirak's magic, and beyond the pulse of these visions.

Instead, I walked—agonizingly slowly, step by weary step—back to the small house I kept at the edge of Wyvern's Court, and there I collapsed into sleep.

CHAPTER 3

"*A*hnmik, *I have always been yours, your voice, your tool. Help me now, I beg you. Give me the strength to do what must be done today.*"

The falcon Cjarsa whispered the prayer as she pushed open the doors of the temple. Araceli was deep in meditation and did not notice the intrusion, even as a shaft of sunlight fell across the altar—a simple black silk melos *scarf draped across cold gray stone, with a single alabaster statue, symbol of the god Ahnmik, on it.*

The rest of the room was equally stark, except for one corner, where a three-year-old child with fair hair slept upon a soft violet cushion. Araceli had found the girl abandoned in the jungle, far from the desert lands of their home, and had named her Alasdair.

Protector.

"*Araceli, it is time.*"

Kiesha, the cobra high priestess of Anhamirak, stood in the doorway to her temple, holding her head high despite her obvious

20

exhaustion. Cjarsa remembered this woman as having mahogany hair, sun-touched skin and brown eyes, but Anhamirak's fire had dyed Kiesha's body as surely as Ahnmik's ice had dyed Cjarsa's. Kiesha's warm earthen eyes had become lakes of blood, and they were no longer kind but eerily piercing as she beheld Cjarsa, whose power had once been the opposite–the balance–of hers.

Many things had changed since Maeve had abandoned their coven. Once, they had been the protectors and leaders of their people, priests and priestesses of the eight great powers, led by Maeve and kept in balance by her guidance. Now the powers were unbalanced.

The stain left on Kiesha's hair and eyes was nothing compared to the terror of the uncontrollable magics that had ripped through each of the Dasi in Maeve's absence. The serpents had blamed the falcons for the first assaults, saying that their worship of death and darkness had led to this destruction; Cjarsa's followers had retaliated, spitting their own accusations against the chaos-worshippers.

"You say you wish to end this," the cobra said to Cjarsa and Araceli in greeting.

"Before more lives are lost," Araceli said.

They had been fighting for years. What else could they do? Anhamirak's domain was wildfire and war. As long as her magic was left unbalanced, there could never be peace.

"Yes," Cjarsa whispered. She had seen the future, seen the final fire that would consume them all. She knew that this had to be stopped. "Come forward, child," she said.

When Alasdair stepped out from behind Araceli and held up a curious hand, Kiesha knelt down and let the tiny fingers wrap around her thumb. "Yours?" she asked Araceli, her expression softening.

"No," Araceli said, blinking back tears. "Brassal killed my

daughter last night. Odd that it would be a priest of Namid, giver of life, who would destroy a child."

The python had crept into Ahnmik's temple, probably hoping to kill Cjarsa. Instead, he had found Araceli and her young daughter.

Araceli was convinced that he had killed the child intentionally; Cjarsa believed it had been an accident. Like all their powers, Brassal's magic had grown beyond his ability to control it.

"Now," Cjarsa whispered, throwing out her own magic like a net. Araceli, Syfka, Servos and Cjarsa had spent the past three years concocting this spell, and now it drove Kiesha to her knees. The cobra screamed.

And the child screamed as well.

Oh, gods . . . hearing that scream, Cjarsa wanted to leave this world. The spell the falcons had created shredded Kiesha's magic, tearing it into two. One half of Anhamirak's power remained in the cobra; the other half burned its way into the child's soul. As it had painted Kiesha garnet, so it stained the child, darkening her white-blond hair and pale blue eyes to the color of beaten gold.

It was too late to bring back the balance, and no one could control Anhamirak's chaos, but they hoped that this would cripple the serpents' magic before it could destroy even more.

Araceli was the one who took the little girl's tiny hands in her own and whispered gently, "Now you'll be able to fly, like we can."

"Don't be kind," Cjarsa said. "If you are kind, we will never be able to do what must be done."

"Come, Alasdair," Araceli said, taking the young hawk's hand before Kiesha could recover and realize what they had done. "You have much to learn before we take you back to your people."

No, this wasn't me. This wasn't my time. All this had happened long before to Cjarsa, before she had raised the island from the sea and become Empress of the white city. I'd seen it before; the first time, I had screamed with Kiesha, screamed for days until Cjarsa had helped me escape the vision.

Where was I . . . oh, there . . .

Even generations later, the Cobrianas' garnet eyes had not faded. As Anjay rode in a fury to the Hawk's Keep, they burned with the same intensity that had made Cjarsa cringe when she had faced Kiesha in the temple of Anhamirak.

Some of Anjay's soldiers had followed him, and they fell by the dozens as he thrust forward into avian lands, but no bow or blade seemed able to pierce his pain and hatred.

The cobra had returned from falcon lands only hours before. He knew nothing of the child he had sired, and if he had been lingering on recollections of the falcon lover he had left behind, those had been shoved aside by the news of his sister's assassination.

Anjay did not dismount as he reached the courtyard of the Hawk's Keep, but boosted himself up to stand on his horse's back; a raven tried to stop him from grasping the balcony floor above, and Anjay quickly drove a blade into the man's ribs.

As Anjay hoisted himself over the balcony rail, a young hawk girl shrieked the raven's name with enough pain in her voice that Anjay knew that the man he had just killed had been her mate. Fine; he would end this hawk's pain, too, as her people had ended the lives of so many he loved.

All the while, the falcon Darien shadowed him, and she let out a cry that echoed the girl's as the youngest avian prince defended his sister, Danica, by driving a soldier's blade into Anjay's back. The avians had lost scores of their own people to this mad rush, and now they cheered as a serpent's blood flowed over the child's hand.

*　*　*

No, no. Why was I forced to watch this, again and again, every time I closed my eyes? I shared Anjay's blood. Did I need to share his death?

And now, finally, I remembered who I was: the unwanted child of a doomed cobra prince, and a falcon sworn to the Empress Cjarsa, who had ripped Anhamirak's magic in half. Had the avians and the serpiente known, all those years as they had warred, that they had slain the other halves of themselves? Was that why peace came with such difficulty: not because they hated each other, but because they could not forgive themselves?

I was a young child, dancing the skies above the white city, lost in the endless tides of magic that whirled through this land like storm winds. The wings I spread showed the taint of my father's blood—the color of tar and lava. Anhamirak's stain.

My father's magic was not powerful; a cobra did not have enough power on his own to be a danger. But when what remained of Anhamirak's magic needled the falcon magic I had inherited from my mother, Ahnmik slashed back. I spent most of my days struggling to control these combinative powers, but in the middle of this sky-dance, I lost that battle.

The two magics fought, tearing and slicing, ripping at my body and my wings. Dark flight feathers cascaded to the ground even before I fell screaming.

Cjarsa caught me before the crystal-hard ground shattered my plummeting body, but though she mended my flesh, she could do nothing with my ravaged wings. As for the rest of me . . . the agony from my magic was as deep as my blood, and even my Empress could not heal that.

24

She cradled me in her arms as I shivered and cried, my magic striking her blindly no matter how I tried to keep it in check.

"Sleep now," she whispered to me. It was all she could do.

Yes, I would have liked to sleep, to rest, to finally be away from the sharp edges left behind by that ancient rending. But . . . I had made a promise. I needed to find my way back to *here* and *now*, in Wyvern's Court, such a strange and unlikely place. The two halves of Anhamirak were trying to shove themselves together, but it was like trying to return blood to a wound.

Back to Wyvern's Court . . .

Salem Cobriana, the heir to the serpiente throne, lay in my arms, dying. His blood felt cold on my skin; his red eyes had turned a tawny brown. His heartbeat was so faint that even with my cheek pressed to his chest I could barely hear it.

I knew I could save him; I had that power, always had. I could use my magic, patch his bones, slow the bleeding, force his heart to beat and his lungs to stir the air . . . but terror gripped me. I could ask my magic for that much, and Ahnmik would grant the favor, but the white falcon's power ultimately came from the void, from Ecl, and that dark goddess would ask even more in return. If I swam her dark, still waters, I would drown. I shrieked for help, but none came.

The mob was seething. How had the crowd turned so vile so quickly?

An arrow pierced my back, slicing under my left shoulder blade. I covered Salem with my body but did not reach out to him with the greedy magic that could save his life. I couldn't. Please . . .

Another arrow sliced through my arm before burying itself in his side.

"Hai!" *Someone shouted my name. At that moment, I felt Salem die, felt the last spark go out as Brysh, goddess of death, claimed her own.*

No, not her own. This wasn't natural; this was a travesty. I screamed and then let the magic free, lashing into the crowd.

Hai!

Shm'Ahnmik'la'Hai. Kiesha'ra'la'Hai.

Pain. Fear. Not from me or from Salem but from someone else, someone who knew all my names.

Stay here, Hai. Stay here, with me.

Only one person ever called me by both sides of my blood: Nicias. He named me shm'Ahnmik, *a falcon, and* Kiesha'ra, *a cobra.*

I wanted the serpent throne no more than Nicias wanted his throne on Ahnmik. We would never claim our royal birthrights, but our magics would forever tie us to them. The words—his bond to me, and mine to him—drew me back to the real world.

CHAPTER 4

I lifted my head, in the place and time most call reality, in the bedroom of my little home at the edge of Wyvern's Court, and found Nicias standing across the room from me, one arm held protectively in front of his face. His forearm was bleeding in four places, as if scratched by the claws of some great cat; I could see a dark stain on his shirt where his chest had been similarly torn. A cloud of angry magic—my magic, which I had lashed out with during my unwanted visions— stormed around him.

I curled into a ball, trying to draw the magic back from Nicias and into myself and knowing that I might have killed anyone else who had woken me. I shut my eyes for a moment and again heard the whisper of Ecl, who for so long had been my keeper . . . my guardian, my kingdom, my ever-jealous lover. Her voice was soothing, and I felt myself falling back into sleep.

Nicias touched my arm, terribly trusting even with blood trickling down his skin. "Hai, stay with me."

"*Quemak*," I said. He had called me a falcon and a cobra, but I was neither really. Opal was right. *Quemak*, mongrel. That was the only title I could claim.

Nicias winced when I said it. The word was not a polite one, and I knew he hated to hear me apply it to myself, but how could he argue? We both knew it was true.

"You're hurting yourself," he said. The magic I had been trying to pull away from him had cut into my own arms instead. I didn't mind the pain much; I was nearly numb to it. But I hated to see blood on his skin.

He gently ran his hands down my arms. I shivered, both at his touch and at the brush of his magic, which felt like cold water in the scalding desert. He smoothed the cuts I had created, transforming them into something harmless that quickly faded.

I doubted that Nicias could explain how he had done it. He had begun to study his falcon magic only within the past few months, but he was royal blood, so his power responded freely to his desires. Simple things like this he could do instinctively.

"Nightmare?" Nicias asked as he healed us both.

How I envied people who dreamed, who could have nightmares and know that in no world were they real.

"*Sakkri.*"

Nicias resented anything resembling prophecy. He had not been raised with the assumption that if one was strong enough, one could look forward in time and see what Fate had planned. Not every *sakkri'a'she*, vision of the future, came true, but every one had the potential to do so.

Few people had the power to weave such *sakkri*, and among those who could, even fewer had the strength to recall them. I was one of the few, but even I had trouble sometimes; I would remember single images or driving desires instead of whole scenes. Most of the time, I let the future-memories fade.

But this time something had caused me to wake screaming and struggling.

I had seen my father killed—no, I saw that frequently, almost every time I slept. It no longer had the power to—

Salem. His was the death that had disturbed me. The memory of it made me shudder. I could almost taste the helpless terror and fury I had felt in the vision . . . *almost.* The emotions were already fading, returning me to my more familiar state of numbness. But surely in the future I had envisioned, I had felt like I was losing something far more dear than one cobra's life. *Why?*

I had once given myself to Ecl to rid myself of these kinds of visions, which were rich with emotions—most often painful ones—that had no parallel in my everyday existence. Now I had taken myself back to reality and was trying to live again. Would this be my punishment, to have this cobra die in my arms while I wept? Would I die with him?

Will I be the cause of his death? I wondered.

"What did you see?" Nicias asked, drawing me from my dark thoughts.

I shook my head; I couldn't speak of it. Describing such prophecies made them more real, and as I had recently experienced with Oliza, sometimes that was enough to set one into motion.

"It doesn't matter. It will fade," I said. At least, I prayed it would.

Nicias sighed and ran his hands through his pale blond

hair, which was hanging loose around his face. The blue strands were tangled with all the rest, and I wished I could reach forward and separate them, binding the golden locks back, the way they would be worn on Ahnmik.

Old habit, left over from years in the white city when I had prayed and wished I could have the pale, pale blond hair of my Empress, marked with a falcon's blue, instead of the black hair of a cobra.

Or perhaps it was a desired habit. Every time Nicias was near, I found myself inventing excuses to touch him.

I kept my hands by my sides.

"I can't stay long," Nicias said apologetically. "The court is—dear skies, you weren't even there. Hai—"

"I heard," I said. "Oliza has given up the throne."

Nicias nodded. "Salem and Sive will inherit the serpiente and avian thrones. Neither of them hates the other. Hopefully . . ."

Hopefully they would be able to maintain the peace between the avians and the serpiente and bring the two worlds together so that someday a wyvern queen might be able to rule. Hopefully the slaughter that had lasted more than a thousand years would never begin again.

"What will Oliza do now?"

"She has taken a wolf for her mate," he said. "A woman named Betia. They left Wyvern's Court as soon as Oliza made the announcement."

It had been obvious to me from the beginning that Oliza loved the wolf. Even so, I nodded, accepting the information as if it was new.

Fate did care for its children sometimes. Long before, Araceli and Cjarsa had split Anhamirak's magic to protect this world. In Oliza, daughter of a hawk and a cobra, that magic had again combined. Love that would never let Oliza breed was a gift, as any natural-born child of the wyvern's would unleash terror on this Earth.

"Salem plans to formally name his mate tomorrow night," Nicias said. "He believes it will comfort his people if he takes the serpiente throne quickly, so they do not need to wonder if he will also step aside. I'm not sure I agree with his reasoning, but . . ." He shook his head. "Salem will be king, and once that is done, it will be harder for Oliza to return if she wants to. I think Salem would step aside if she tried, but a king cannot give up his crown as easily as an heir can give up her birthright." He let out a frustrated sound. "I don't like this. Oliza has gone off and asked none of her guard to follow her. Salem's mother is still exploring *somewhere,* and though we've sent dozens of messengers for Irene, there is no guarantee they will find her. We've spent most of the last two months trying to control riots in the marketplace, and now, with Oliza gone, it is going to be even harder. It isn't a good time for the royal house to be so scattered." Nicias shook his head again. "I'm sorry. I don't mean to burden you with this."

Nicias usually tried to shelter me from what he perceived as the more difficult aspects of this reality, as if any bad news might send me back into Ecl. Perhaps someday it would, but not right now. I attempted to find something to say that would encourage him to continue the conversation.

She and some wolf have run off in the woods together, leaving Salem and Sive holding the bag, Gren had said. Since Oliza's mate did not care for other wolves, they could be with only one group: the Obsidian guild. The guild, which included

Maeve's descendents, was shunned equally by serpiente and falcons. Though they had been pardoned by the Cobriana two generations before, very few of them had elected to rejoin serpiente society.

"Oliza is safe," I assured Nicias. The leader of the Obsidian guild had introduced himself to me within days of my waking in Wyvern's Court. He was another of my late father's devotees, and he had made it clear that I was always welcome in the Obsidian camp. Though only a child when Anjay had died, the white viper spoke highly of the long-dead cobra and had even implied once that the outlaw guild might have returned to ally with the rest of the serpiente if my father had survived to rule. I would not call him a friend, but I was familiar with his ways. He would not allow a traveling dancer to be threatened in his land. "I know where she was heading, and you don't need to worry about her there."

Nicias and I never spoke the word *Obsidian* between us, but I sensed he knew both of my connection with that guild and of Oliza's. My neglecting to give specifics now was enough to tell him who Oliza was with.

"She will always be my queen . . . and I will always protect her, as long as she will allow me to," Nicias said. "I know she doesn't want a guard loitering around her, but it would make me—and the rest of her guards, not to mention her family—feel worlds better if I could see for myself that she is safely settled."

I shook my head. "You wouldn't be welcome." A glimpse of a royal guard would make the entire guild disappear.

"No, of course not. You're right."

"You need to stay in the court, anyway," I said. Then,

noticing his troubled expression, I added, "If you would like, I can check on the wyvern."

"Thank you. You don't know how much it would mean to me."

Yes, I do, I thought.

"I need to go," Nicias said. "I shouldn't have stayed even this long."

I sent him a silent query, by magic instead of voice. At his sharp look, I repeated myself out loud. "Why *did* you come here?"

"I felt you scream." His voice was soft.

But why come to my side? I asked silently. *Why do you do all this for me when you know I am only a danger to you, a mongrel falcon in your world of serpents and avians?*

He ignored my silent words, as he always did. I knew he heard me, but he would only acknowledge my questions if I pronounced them.

"Thank you," I said instead.

"Will you be all right?"

"I will be fine," I answered. "I shan't dissolve away—and I will bring back news of your queen."

He kissed my cheek. "Take care of yourself, Hai."

"Teska-Kaya'ga'la."

He gave me a curious look when I used the endearment, which meant *my light*. He knew he was. My vow to him was what kept me in this world, kept me from the numbing darkness of Ecl.

"O'hena-sorma'la'lo'Mehay," he replied. Literally, the title meant *sister of my soul*, though, like most of the old language, it had many different connotations. Some were fraternal; others were more loving, closer to *soulmate*.

He did not explain what he meant any more than I had explained what I'd said. Instead, he went back to Wyvern's Court, to continue his exhausting struggle against the future—a future he still believed he could control, though I feared we might all soon drown.

CHAPTER 5

I followed Nicias to the front door. As we hesitated on the threshold, my eyes lingered on him in a way I could not have avoided had I tried, and for a moment I was transported to another time, another place, where this man was not Nicias Silvermead but Nicias of Ahnmik—son of the *aona*, the Empress's heir, Araceli.

The aona'ra *walked upon paths that rippled with power, two of his Mercy beside him. Nicias's footsteps were soft and echoed by music; the white city embraced its only prince, its spirits cajoling him, gossiping with him and praying to him as he passed.*

He had nearly learned not to weep at the road's bittersweet songs, which conveyed the tears of all those who had lost their loved ones to powers like Ecl.

Hai had once spoken a prophecy to him. She had made him swear never to betray Oliza, and informed him that there could be no future in which he took the white throne of Ahnmik and Oliza survived to rule Wyvern's Court. What Hai had not said was that Oliza would choose to give up her throne, regardless of the choices he made.

"Hai?" Nicias called me back to reality once more, with worry in his ice blue eyes.

"Nicias . . . what will you do now, without Oliza?"

"The Diente and the Tuuli Thea have asked the Wyvern guard to stay in the court for now," he answered. "Many of us have been offered positions with the Royal Flight or the serpiente palace guard, should we wish them in the case we are eventually dissolved."

He still protected Oliza; he always would.

He wished only that he could be numb to the crying. . . .

He had gone into the Halls of shm'Ecl *once, intending to do what Cjarsa and Araceli refused to do. Royal blood called to the* shm'Ecl; *he could save them, like he had saved Hai.*

He had tried.

But this time he had failed, and though he had survived, three members of his Mercy–three falcons who had willingly chosen to serve him, to protect him–had lost their lives. Their deaths had taken something Ecl had not been able to, a shard of . . . something he couldn't find words for.

Oh . . . gods.

Your soul, my love, I cried to the ghost of a Nicias I prayed would never exist. *Your soul, your compassion. That is what you lost with their deaths.*

He wasn't thinking of returning to Ahnmik—was he?

"You've mentioned the plans for the Wyverns. I was asking about *you*. Will you stay in Wyvern's Court?" I asked, somewhat desperately. *I* longed for the white city, but the falcon land wasn't for Nicias. Ahnmik would destroy him. It nearly had before; it would for certain if he went back there.

"I imagine so."

If he, like my mother, believed that he could do the most good from the white city, no power on this earth would stop him. Prophecy certainly would not.

He looked at me with concern. "What's wrong?"

I shook my head. "Nothing. Just—nothing." Nothing that words would help. "You need to get back."

He nodded slowly, those blue eyes gazing into mine, before finally turning away. I watched him shapeshift into the beautiful peregrine falcon that was his second form. As he spread wing and shot into the sky, my breath stilled. How I wanted to do the same.

Instead, I saddled Najat, the Arabian mare that the serpiente royal house had given me, and headed into the woods.

Though the Obsidian camp moved constantly, I never had trouble finding it. White vipers had little active power, but Maeve's magic was like a beacon to me.

The first "sentry" I saw around Obsidian land was not a guard but a child who could not have been more than four years old. Concerned that she might be lost, I dismounted Najat and walked slowly toward her.

"Hello?"

The child, who was intently peering through the trees, did not seem to hear me.

"Hello?" I said again, moving closer.

The girl turned toward me, her eyes wide. Though her milk-fair hair spoke of white-viper parentage, her eyes were a deep, rusty red: a cobra's eyes. My first thought was *Another of my father's?*

Absurd—my father had been dead two and a half decades—but she was obviously the result of some cobra's indiscretion. I doubted that Oliza's father would have strayed from his beloved Naga, which left only Salem. I had not thought that a boy so tightly bound to the dancer's nest would wander into these woods, but how well did I really know my cousin?

"Are you lost?" I asked when the girl didn't speak. "Do you know how to get back to your family?"

She chewed on her lower lip.

"Here, take my hand," I said softly. "I'll help you get back to the camp."

She raised her tiny hand to put it into mine, and only then did I see the blood on her pale skin.

"Are you hurt—"

I had only half finished the question when she wrapped her fingers around my hand and the world shattered.

Fire.

I shrieked as a wyvern's untamed power tore through me, searing everything that Ahnmik had left frozen and numb and ripping from me all the *sakkri* I had ever spun.

I saw Wyvern's Court awash in scalding magic. Serpents and avians slaughtered by Oliza's child—*this* child, Keyi, who didn't exist yet, except in visions like this one. She looked different every time I saw her, but each time, the vision was so powerful I had no way to guard myself from it.

Oh, gods. I could see . . .

The survivors fighting as the falcons came to try to tame An-hamirak's power before it could engulf the whole world as it nearly had once before.

So much screaming, so much pain.

Nicias, weeping as if his heart had been ripped from him.

And then I recalled the moment, months before, when Nicias had dove into Ecl to save me and had nearly lost himself. I told him: *I have danced a thousand futures and lived a thousand lifetimes, and all I have seen are ashes and ice. You are too– You don't belong here. You have things to do, out there. Go, Nicias,* please.

Only if you will.

Swear you'll go back, and I'll try.

I couldn't stand to see Nicias fall in that dark place, but surely he would have found his way back. I could have said no. Instead . . .

I swear.

Then I swear as well.

Why had I made that vow? This world *hurt.* Everything was a struggle, without the possibility of any end but fire. Did these fools really think their mixed-blood world had any hope?

I tried to shove away the visions.

Hai? Nicias's silent concerned query reached me from Wyvern's Court. *Are you all right?*

I couldn't have him come here, this close to Obsidian land. *I'm fine,* I replied. *I'm fine, I'm fine, I'm fine.*

Are you sure–

I'm fine!

I severed the communication, one word pounding in time with my pulse: *why why why why why why?*

Why had I tied myself back to this world? I could have remained in the Halls of *shm'Ecl* for a thousand years and more, and I would never have needed to know this pain.

I had almost broken free of the *sakkri* when someone real touched my shoulder, upsetting my power yet again.

"*Nasa-Vere-nas'ka'la!*" Don't touch me! I commanded, lashing out at the white viper with my magic.

He fell back, his moss green eyes hot with fear and anger. The members of the Obsidian guild shared their names only with those they trusted most, but my power had found the viper's name—Vere—and now it was twisted into the magic that was digging like thorns into his skin.

"Remove it," he whispered to me.

I reached out to do so, and my whole body shuddered. "I can't."

He moved closer and reached toward me again but stopped with his fingertips an inch from my skin as my magical command made his muscles freeze.

"Are you all right?" he asked.

Was *I* all right? I had wrapped the leader of the Obsidian guild in falcon magic, and now he asked me if I was all right. He should have been cursing me.

"I'm—"

Again I caught sight of the girl, further back in the woods, but this time I recognized her for what she was: a *sakkri*. A vision of horror wrapped in a child's innocent form.

"Skies above," I whispered, dropping my head into my hands. "Not again."

In most futures in which Oliza took the throne, peace ended with an assassin's blade. In the handful of futures in which Oliza lived long enough to bear Keyi, the child slew her mother and destroyed most of Wyvern's Court before the falcons descended to pick up remnants of the once grand society.

I had often seen the look in my mother's eye as she realized that my Empress had been right all along in creating the avian-serpiente war to protect them from this rampant magic. Many times, I had wondered how that horror would manifest itself in her opinion of her daughter. Would she be proud that I, a mongrel, had been loyal when even her faith had wavered?

Or would I simply be a reminder of yet another disastrous mistake?

Would I still find the answer to that question? Oliza had abdicated. She did not plan to have natural-born children. Why was the vision of Keyi still coming to me so strongly?

I felt Obsidian struggle against the magic I had left on him, and shift it until he could lay a cautious hand on my shoulder.

"Talk to me," he said.

"Fire," I whispered. I squeezed my eyes shut against the image. "It's too much. I can't control it."

"Can't control what?"

"*Everything.* The future."

"No one can," he said.

The anguish I felt wasn't my own. It belonged to the serpents and the avians who would be destroyed in a future in which this child existed. Even so, it felt as if my heart had been ripped from me. . . .

Suddenly, for the first time since the day I had spun my first *sakkri,* I was weeping. I cried without tears and without sound, but still my breath hitched and my body shook. I reached for Ecl, my peaceful oblivion, but this close to Maeve's kin and the balancing magic they still held, I couldn't make myself fall into the void even if I could have forgotten that damning vow to Nicias.

Without words, Obsidian wrapped me in his arms, holding me as I struggled to free myself from the aching sorrow. Was this how other people felt, all the time? How could anyone live if at any moment they could be struck by this pain? Even when I shoved back all the screaming, wailing and weeping, I could taste tears on the back of my tongue and feel them making my lungs tight and my chest heavy.

Finally, as the dry sobs subsided, I asked, "Why?"

"Why what?"

"Why comfort a mongrel falcon who would strike you with magic just for coming near?"

He tilted his head, a quizzical, almost amused expression on his face. "You really don't know?"

"You've said you were loyal to my father," I said, guessing.

"True, I was loyal to Anjay Cobriana. If he had lived to be king, I would have followed him. When you first came to Wyvern's Court, I introduced myself to you because I knew you were his daughter. But that is not why I am still here right now."

"Then why?"

He shook his head as he rose to his feet, and offered me a hand to help me stand. "I would never be able to walk away from someone in the condition I found you in. I don't have a falcon's power, but I could feel your agony half a mile away."

When he saw my confusion, he asked, "Doesn't anyone on Ahnmik ever just do the right thing?"

I snickered. "*Right* is a relative term when you're dealing with the white falcon."

Hesitantly, I took Vere Obsidian's hand, but this time there was no flash of power. No visions overwhelmed me as I rose shakily to my feet; I was too burned out for even my volatile magic to catch a spark.

CHAPTER 6

"I've never thought of you as a falcon until now," Vere said, "when I heard you speak of yourself as if Anhamirak has never touched you. I suppose it was arrogant of me, to ignore one half of your parentage because I was fonder of the other."

"If you have to ignore half my blood, I would rather you ignore my father's," I said, cut by his words, which I had heard in many forms as a child.

He shook his head. "Then you would have been dead long before I let you walk these woods."

"I could kill you before you could injure me," I pointed out. "I could kill you in such a way that you would feel like it took you centuries to die. I was raised on Ahnmik, after all. I might have been a dancer, but I learned many of the Mercy's tricks."

He nodded. "I suppose you could, except for one thing."

"What is that?"

"You would have to care enough about your own life, and my death, to do it. And you don't, not nearly."

I shrugged. "Perhaps."

Perhaps. I felt very tired, very worn down by the despair in my visions, for someone who couldn't care less if she lived or died.

As if summoned by my thoughts, the child darted across our path again. White-blond hair streamed behind the running figure.

"I told Nicias I would check on Oliza for him," I said, shifting the topic to something that concerned me more, "since I knew that you would not want him to come here himself." Partly I spoke to fulfill my duty to the peregrine, but I was equally interested in learning Vere's opinion of the abdicated princess. Keyi's possible fathers were many, but her white-blond hair in this particular vision could come only from one of the white vipers of the Obsidian guild.

"She's here. Heartbroken by what she has had to do, but confident that it was the right thing. Betia will help her through it." He paused, considering, before he added, "I have no objection to her being our guest, but I would like someday to know why she made the decision she did. I haven't wanted to pressure her."

"And you think I might know?"

"I *know* you know," he replied. "It's only a matter of whether you'll tell me."

"When your kin first left the Dasi, do you know what happened?"

"I suspect you're going to tell me I don't," he said wryly.

"In the ancient days, the Dasi were able to summon spirits for guidance and call the rains to feed their crops.

Namid's priest could see if a mother was kindled with life just by looking at her, and when it was time, he could usher that life into the world with ease. Brysh's priestess could take a dying man's last breath just as painlessly and wrap the survivors in peaceful mourning. When your ancestor Maeve left the Dasi, all control, all balance, left with her. Rains turned to floods that swept away homes and drowned dozens of men, women and children." *A bassinet, swept down the river, with a wailing infant inside.* "Namid's touch could burn a woman so the life inside her bled. Just a glance from the aplomado Syfka—who had been sworn to Brysh—could make a person fall, and a glance from Kiesha, Anhamirak's priestess . . ." I shuddered. "Can you imagine a cobra's being able to kindle fire with those garnet eyes?"

"They nearly can still," Vere whispered.

"Serpents don't remember what it was like in those first days, but I've seen it. If somehow Oliza and her mate survived her coronation—an unlikely enough possibility, since serpents will not accept an avian Nag, and avians will not accept a serpent alistair—Oliza's child would bring back those days of despair, which the entire avian-serpiente war was fought to keep at bay."

The war. Nicias felt that the falcons' actions had been unjust, that kindling the war had been evil, but what else could have been done, when there were no good decisions that could have been made?

"How can you know this?" Vere asked me.

"*Sakkri,*" I replied.

Why was I trying to warn this white viper of what the consequences might be if he or one of his people joined with Oliza? What did I have to lose if Wyvern's Court burned? It would possibly mean my reconciliation with my mother, and therefore my Empress, presuming I survived the fire.

It would mean Nicias's broken heart as well.

And of course, the loss of Wyvern's Court.

Our conversation was interrupted as we reached the Obsidian campsite, and I was grateful for the timing. It kept me from pondering why I found myself trying to protect Wyvern's Court when letting it burn might gain me everything.

The Obsidian camp was simple. Hammocks, designed so they could be taken down swiftly if necessary, had been strung between the trees around a central fire. The Obsidian guild was tolerated by the current monarchy, but in the past they had been actively hunted, and they had never dropped their habits from those days. All their camps were transient, and all their members armed.

As we entered, a pair of serpents was performing a flame-dance. They wove their bodies against each other, sliding around, over and through the campfire.

A mistake, and those watching would choke on the smell of burned flesh.

I closed my eyes, and for a moment I saw the triple arches of Ahnmik. The three arches were among the highest structures in the city, less only to the *yenna'marl*, the white towers. To fall from that height . . .

Some days, I felt as if I might still be falling.

I opened my eyes, forcing my attention past the dancers, to where Oliza was curled in the arms of her wolf, Betia. The wyvern's eyes were swollen, as if she had been crying, and she was watching the flame-dance intently, as if to avoid drowning in her own thoughts. Her expression, which reflected how I felt every moment of my waking life, drew me to her almost against my will.

Betia saw me first, and her gaze met mine. *Don't hurt her,* the wolf said, quite clearly, without needing to speak. *She has been through enough today.* I nodded, knowing she would sooner snap my neck than let me harm her mate.

Betia's attention prompted Oliza's, and the wyvern visibly braced herself as she watched me approach.

I almost said, *I understand.* I knew why Oliza had left, knew the horrors she had seen, which no one should ever have to face. I was probably the only person in this world who fully understood.

But as I looked into Oliza's eyes, the words fled. The once princess had her mate for understanding. She had Obsidian land for sanctuary. And, I realized, she had the blessed amnesia that came to those who worked *sakkri* without training. She remembered only enough to know that she had chosen this exile for a reason, and to fear the woman who had twice triggered the terrifying visions of the future.

I took a step back, surprised by how much it hurt to see such wariness in her.

"I'm sorry," I said, without being able to help it.

"Why?" Oliza's voice was guarded, with good reason. She had no way of knowing that I had not intentionally shown her the visions that had eventually led to her abdication.

Araceli, heir to the Empress, had hinted more than once that it would please the royal falcon house if Oliza never took the throne of Wyvern's Court. If the veiled request had come from Cjarsa, or if my loyalty to Nicias had not stayed my hand, I would not have hesitated to sabotage Oliza's reign.

Oliza was right to be nervous. She had no reason to trust me.

"For intruding," I said. "Nicias was worried. Since he can't come here, I told him I would look in on you."

Oliza relaxed a little when I said the peregrine's name. "Please, thank Nicias for checking on me, and tell him that I'm sorry I couldn't let him know where I was going. I'm with friends." She added, "I couldn't stay at court."

"He understands." *As do I.* "I'll let him know you are safe."

"Thank you."

I turned to go, but she called my name.

"Hai?"

"Yes?"

"I know my leaving hurt Nicias. Take care of him?"

The image of Nicias as Ahnmik's cold prince briefly flickered through my memory. I wondered if Oliza had seen that vision, and if it had made any difference. "I will, as long as I can."

I walked away from Oliza and Betia and back toward the dancers.

Watching their movement, I could almost read the pattern left by the dancers' bodies. The white vipers currently performing had just enough magic to lace the air with innate power but not enough to hold the spell in place. Otherwise, a *daraci'Kain* like this would have had the power to call the rain . . . or, if unbalanced, to drown the earth.

"What do you think of our dancers?" Vere Obsidian asked me.

I shook my head, trying to banish the image of dancing from my mind . . . trying to forget the white arches, where I had experienced the greatest bliss and the greatest devastation.

"They're lovely," I said, with no real emotion in my voice.

The dancers had sunk into a deep bow, feet, knees, head and hands pressed to the ground. There were two reasons for the bow: the first was to give thanks to the audience, and the second was to recover their strength.

On Ahnmik, such a bow would sometimes last days, as the dancers rested. Those dances were rare, but incredible to behold, especially when performed by someone of the upper ranks.

"Hai?"

"What?" I snapped, more forcefully than I had intended.

Vere Obsidian held out his hand. "Dance with me."

Fool. Didn't he know my wings were broken? They had been scarred, tortured and lost the *last* time I had tried to dance, in the skies of the white city. "Are you still courting my father, Vere, or are you courting me now?"

He arched an eyebrow. "I might do both," he admitted, "if I thought I could ever mean half as much to you as your peregrine does. But what man on this earth could hope to compete with the prince who brought you back to life?"

The honest reply, so blunt that it could have come only from a serpent, diminished my useless anger. I just shook my head. "I don't dance anymore." I rubbed my hands over my arms, smoothing away goose bumps. "Please, just . . . understand."

"It's hard to understand when you refuse to explain."

Serpents! Only they would insist on dragging such pain back into reality, on rehashing and sharing such vile histories.

He waited, until I found words that could answer him. "The ancient dances were meant to weave magic. I can't control my power even when I do not call upon it; if I try to dance, I don't know what will happen."

"There's more," he said softly, no doubt reading the deeper fear in my eyes.

"Another day, viper."

He sighed. "As you wish . . . cobra."

I winced as I turned away.

Better to forget.

CHAPTER 7

In desperate need of comfort but not wanting to bother Nicias, I traveled to a still pool deeper in the forest. To detach myself from the chaos of this reality, I immersed myself in the cold water. I swam deeper, until my lungs burned and my heart raced, and then finally those physical pains faded as my magic replaced breath and blood.

I reached for the city of Ahnmik.

My two mothers—Darien, who had borne me, and Cjarsa, who had raised me—were almost always together and were almost always fighting. Few people had the power or the courage to argue with the Empress Cjarsa, but Darien was one of those rare souls who did.

I did not mean to intrude on their conversation that day, but I had carelessly reached too far. Cjarsa and Darien ceased talking and shifted their attention to me.

"Hai?" my mother said.

The instant Darien spoke my name, Cjarsa turned away,

assuming that I was not seeking her. Losing that brief moment of attention from my Empress was like having all sunlight disappear. I knew that Darien sensed my reaction; I felt her disappointment through the magic that connected us in that moment.

What did she expect from me, the daughter she had abandoned?

If my devotion had been focused on anyone but Cjarsa, would Darien have cared at all? Or was this just another excuse for her war with my Empress? Darien said she wanted to change the island; like Maya, she had lofty ideas, many of which I might have agreed with if I had believed her stated motives. However, as far as I could tell, what motivated my mother was not the desire for equality and freedom of which she spoke but stubborn spite.

I often wondered: If it had truly been love for my father that had driven her to commit treason, wouldn't she have been more concerned about that man's child?

"If you hate the white city and everything it stands for as much as you say you do," I asked my mother bitterly, "if you hate the Lady and her heir and Ahnmik, why do you stay there?"

Why do you stay in that land, that land I have always wanted . . . that land I will never have because I was born with a cobra's blood? Why do you struggle in a place you hate, *struggle and fight, when nothing will ever change?* Why?

Why could you never just be a mother to your daughter?

"Because . . ." Darien tried to explain. Did she herself understand it? Or was this fight just something she had started one day and now couldn't find her way out of? "I love it as much as I hate it."

"I have always only loved it."

"I would give it to you if I knew how. I *am* trying, Hai. I want to change things. As long as I stay here, I have the Empress's ear. I can make things better. Maybe someday you will feel welcome in the city and will come home."

"You don't do this for me."

"I do it for you, and for the Cobriana, and Wyvern's Court, and all the thousands who died in Cjarsa's war. I cannot give you the white city, but I am doing all I can to protect the world you have. You know that Araceli would see Wyvern's Court destroyed if our Empress let her."

"Our" Empress. Only when it suited her purposes.

Still . . .

The child Alasdair's scream.

Blood on the hawk child's hands.

Blood on my own.

"And Oliza's abdication?" I asked. "Did you know of that?"

"The wyvern's magic disrupts my *sakkri*," Darien replied. "I have trouble seeing what she will do. Her abdication was as much a shock to me as it was to you. It certainly was not something I had planned."

"What about Araceli? Or Cjarsa?"

"Neither of them had a hand in it. I have enough power here to keep them from meddling . . . mostly." My mother hesitated. "Did they speak to you?" she asked, no doubt questioning my loyalty, as Oliza did.

"Of course," I replied. Let her take from that what she would; I owed this woman no answers. There was only one reason I wished to have her as an ally. "Regardless, my concern isn't for Oliza. I'm worried about Nicias, now that he isn't bound to her. You helped him leave the island once—"

I broke off, suddenly realizing that Darien was not on my side. She had helped Nicias leave the island, yes, but she had always wanted him beside her on Ahnmik.

"If you take Nicias from here . . ." There was no threat that would matter to my mother. I would never forgive her, but since when had she cared?

"Don't you see?" Darien argued. "Nicias has no place in Wyvern's Court—not now—and he could do so much good here. Araceli would listen to Nicias, because she wants her son's favor, and as prince, he would have power I can never dream of."

"My Empress," I said, petitioning for Cjarsa's attention. "Please, leave Nicias alone."

"It is not my will that would bring Nicias here," Cjarsa replied. "I have denied both Darien and Araceli permission to interfere with him. However, if he comes home of his own free will, I cannot refuse him his place."

"There is no free will. Not on Ahnmik."

"I will not take him from you," my Empress assured me. It was a cold comfort, and she knew it; she probably would not need to. "Be strong, *quemak'nesera*," she bid me, the words a dismissal.

My mother said nothing as I severed the magic between us so abruptly that I fell into the sound of Nicias's screams.

Oliza's child, Keyi, was laughing, her red-blond hair rippling around her cherubic face. Her eyes were bright and as golden as a hawk's, but her eyelashes were pitch-black, an eerie contrast to her otherwise fair features. Her hands and arms were stained by twisting indigo magic that contorted and heaved across her flesh, but the child paid it no mind.

Keyi laughed. She was too young to understand ruin.

Sive Shardae wore not a mark upon her skin, but she was as still and silent as all Brysh's realm as Araceli lifted Aleya into her arms.

Sive's baby began to wail.

"You can't take Aleya!"

Keyi giggled as Nicias protested and struggled to reclaim the only surviving heir to the Tuuli Thea. The falcons had taken Salem's son Zenle; they couldn't take Aleya.

Araceli's Mercy held Nicias back, two of them gripping each of his arms.

Araceli held the baby as gently as porcelain, looking sadly into its frightened eyes. "I will return her to the avian throne when the time comes," she assured Nicias. "Be grateful . . . my grandson . . . that I do not have the heart to slay my own blood." She dropped her gaze to Keyi, who had begun to hum a little song. "Care for that one, if you wish. I will leave to you the decision of when she must be given back to Brysh."

"No," he pleaded.

Araceli turned with Aleya in her arms, and again Nicias shrieked, tearing into the guards holding him physically and magically. They knocked him to his knees as black-red slices of power rent his skin, leaving him shuddering on the ground. He could only watch as the falcons carried the little child away.

All of Nicias's monarchs were gone. Aleya and Zenle, taken. Oliza, Salem, Sive, Zane, Danica, Irene . . . The faces of the dead marched through his pained memory.

Keyi still laughed, though her hands—those tiny pink hands—were stained with the blood of thousands. She giggled, reaching for things only she could see: birds and butterflies, faeries and nymphs, raindrops, snowflakes, anything but the steel-hard sky, bleached as white as bone.

*　　*　　*

I dragged myself from the vision, choking on screams as I struggled back to shore.

Don't cry, my love; you do all you can. I wept as I lay on the beach, too exhausted to move. *I'll do what I can, for you.*

Someone nudged my shoulder, roughly checking for life, and my body shuddered and began coughing up water, seeking air instead of raw power to sustain us.

Velyo Frektane looked at me with distaste. One of the two competing alpha wolves in the area, Velyo despised weakness. Nearly drowning in still water probably did not strike him as strong.

"I've heard that falcons can do that—just stop moving, eating, drinking," he remarked. "But I didn't know they could stop breathing."

"Breath belongs to *Mehay*," I replied, drawing in the air nonetheless. I could sustain myself for years on nothing but Ahnmik's power, as I had in the Halls of *shm'Ecl* before Nicias had taken me from there, but if I wanted to escape from that last vision, I needed to ground myself back to the world. "Ecl has no use for it."

The wolf let out a disdainful snort. "Well, sorry to interrupt your melodramatic expiration, but I thought Wyvern's Court might object to a dead cobra in our woods."

I would be shocked if they noticed.

But I accepted the wolf's help as I stood. When I touched his hand, I tried to ignore the images that it conjured. Oliza and her mate had each crossed paths with Velyo in the past.

"Do you need assistance back to Wyvern's Court?"

"I can make it."

He watched me skeptically as I wrung water from my hair; surely I looked less than capable to him, with my hair and clothes still dripping and my hands and arms streaked with dirt from my lying on the ground.

I was content not to earn the high regard of Velyo Frektane. He was a man who was used to power and getting his way even if it meant abusing those beneath him. I was too much a falcon to tolerate intimidation by or force from a wolf and—though I cringed to think it—too much a serpent to forgive the crimes he had committed in his past. After I'd chosen to ignore Araceli's hinted requests that I begin a war in Wyvern's Court shortly after I first woke here, it would have been a pity to start one accidentally by killing a wolf king.

So I walked away, not upset to hear the wolf scoff as I made a halfhearted attempt to brush mud from my skin and clothes.

Wondering if I would have to walk back to Wyvern's Court, I called silently for Najat and was pleased to find that the horse was not too far away in the woods. She came to me, and I climbed into the saddle and closed my eyes to rest as we returned slowly to Wyvern's Court. Najat knew the way home, far better than I.

CHAPTER 8

The ride to Wyvern's Court seemed unnaturally long as I fought fatigue. I intended to tell Nicias that I had seen Oliza, and then I hoped to curl up somewhere to sleep.

I jumped as the peregrine dove through the treetops and returned to human form barely a breath from Najat's side. I expected Nicias to inquire immediately about Oliza, but his first words were "Are you all right?"

I nodded, pleasantly surprised by the query. "I spoke to Oliza. She and Betia are safe with friends who would never let welcome guests be hurt on their land. Oliza asked me to thank you for your concern and assure you that she would be fine."

Nicias reached out as I spoke, and brushed a streak of dirt from my cheek. The brief touch made my skin tingle.

"Thank you for going; it's good to know she is well. Are you *sure* you're all right?" I must have looked puzzled, because he added, "I don't know exactly what happened to you earlier, but I felt enough to worry."

"I didn't mean to trouble you. I know you have more to worry about than me," I said.

He winced. "I'm sorry."

"It wasn't a criticism."

"I know you didn't mean it to be, but I *do* feel responsible for you, and I feel like I've neglected—"

I held up a hand to stop him, before he could go further. "Nicias, I am an adult woman. Not a child. You pulled me from Ecl, and I—at least sometimes—thank you for that, but have you forgotten that I came back to save *your* life? You aren't my caretaker. And I don't want to be your ward."

I took a step back, horrified by what I had just said. Every heated word was true; of all the things I wished I could be to the peregrine, child was not one of them.

But to speak that way to Nicias . . .

When I forced myself to look up at him again, he was regarding me in a way I couldn't quite interpret. "You're right," he said after a few moments. "You're a long way from being helpless. I know that. But I can still care about you, even if you don't need me to."

"I . . ." I didn't know how to respond to that. I tried, haltingly, to explain. "The visions have been more difficult to control of late. There is too much going on. People are making decisions, *major* decisions, and every time they do . . ." I shuddered. "It's hard."

"Because of Oliza's abdication."

I nodded.

"What have you seen?" Nicias asked.

I shook my head. "Nothing specific enough that you could guard against it; I shouldn't even have mentioned it without knowing more."

Nicias looked at me as if he was trying to read my mind. If he did try, he might succeed, but the peregrine was a gentleman, and his own morals kept his magic from violating the privacy of my thoughts.

I reached forward and touched his arm.

"You should rest," I said, feeling the exhaustion in his limbs and realizing that he had been awake not just one night but many. "Your body hasn't learned yet how to go so long without sleep."

Nicias nodded, and I felt him sway slightly as if accepting for the first time how tired he was.

You can invite me to join you, I called mentally. *I wouldn't say no. I would carry you to sweet sleep . . . and perhaps I could find the same in your arms, unhaunted by Ecl.*

Nicias pulled away as he nodded again.

"You're right. I'm no good to anyone in this shape, least of all my . . . king."

I knew he had wanted to say *my queen.*

"Sweet dreams," I bid. Silently, I added, *Sweet dreams, my light, my heart.*

Once he had left, I did not know where to go. One of my father's traits had bred true; like a serpent, I did not do well with silent solitude. If I closed my eyes now, I knew I would see Keyi again. The child frightened me more than anything else in this world could.

I chose the candle shop on the northern hills.

Opal greeted me in the back room with a scowl, but the falcon didn't ask questions as I approached him; he never did. We didn't speak as he wrapped his arms around my waist, savoring the flavor of my magic and the scent of my skin.

It was a false comfort, an illusion, like so much of

Ahnmik's domain, but for now, being in someone's arms as I closed my eyes was enough. For a handful of hours, I slept deeply.

But then, again . . .

Salem Cobriana, Diente, lay in my arms, dying. His body was cold; his red eyes had turned a tawny brown; his heartbeat raced, pushing the poison faster, deeper, while his lungs fought paralysis. I could barely feel him, his life, anymore. Slipping away.

I knew I could save him; I had that power, always had. I could use my magic to heal the tissues, destroy the poison . . . but terror gripped me. I could ask the magic for that much, and she would grant the favor, but she would ask even more in return. I could swim her dark, still waters, but I would drown. I shrieked for help, but none came.

None ever had; none ever would.

I covered Salem with my body, wishing I could give him my warmth, but did not reach out to him with the greedy magic that could save his life. I couldn't. Please . . .

Too late, Nicias reached his fallen monarch's side. He did what I would not, reaching out with his magic, but the attempt was clumsy. He had never had this type of training . . . and it was too late, anyway.

I felt Salem die, felt the last spark go out as Brysh claimed her own.

I woke alone, despite having drifted into sleep in Opal's arms. He had not left long before—the bed was still warm where his body had lain—but it was long enough for that grisly vision of Salem to seep back into my mind.

It had changed. The cobra died of poison now, instead of at the hands of an angry mob.

The end result remained the same.

It was possible that Salem's death called to me so strongly simply because he was a cobra, as my father had been, but I feared there was more to it. To have such a vivid vision twice implied that it was more than a vague, far-off possibility. Fate, or more likely a conspirator, was actively working toward this future.

Fighting Fate was a pursuit for far stronger souls than mine.

The candle shop was quiet as I stepped into the front room. Opal, his hair still tousled from bed, glanced at me but did not even bother to say good morning. Gren and Spark were absent, probably tending their booth in the market, but Maya was there, keeping the fire hot and the tallow soft as she worked.

"I suppose you know that Salem Cobriana takes the throne tonight," Maya said, making it clear that she had not forgotten our argument.

Neither had I. "Gods and Fate willing, he will."

Maya scoffed. "Hai, you—"

"I could never become Diente with Salem Cobriana alive," I said bluntly. If Fate had destined that Salem Cobriana die, there was nothing I could do, but I would not let Wyvern's Court—Nicias's home, *my* home now—fall because this traitor had delusions of a bright new world. "If he falls and I suspect that you had a hand in it, my first order as queen will be to execute the four of you for treason."

In the frozen silence that followed my words, I picked up a small knife that Maya had been using to trim the wicks for her next batch of candles. As she watched with wide eyes, I drew the blade across the back of my hand, not wincing as I cut Ahnmik's symbol into my skin.

"This I swear by blood and blade and flame," I whispered. "To the god Ahnmik who holds all vows true. If Salem Cobriana falls, those responsible will know my wrath."

With a flick of my wrist, I let the droplets of blood that had gathered on my skin splash into the fire. Maya and Opal both recoiled as the flames turned indigo for an instant before collapsing again. As Maya had said, *they* were both *kajaes; they* had no power.

I was not as harmless.

"Do you hear me, Maya?"

She nodded mutely, her gaze locked on the wound on my hand, and the drops of blood there.

"And you will make my will clear to the others?"

"Yes," she whispered.

I wiped the knife on my arm, leaving a streak of blood there as I cleaned the blade. I had done what I could. Without another word, I stepped out of the house, with no plans ever to return.

CHAPTER 9

I watched from the hillside as the people of Wyvern's Court prepared for Salem's coronation. From dawn to dusk, the air reeked of tension, fear, hope and despair, and the sweat of desperate excitement. I knew that the people felt abandoned by Oliza, and though they loved the cobra prince, they had been hurt badly enough that there was an edge of wariness in their jubilation as they gathered in the market square to witness the young dancer's rise to king.

By evening, all the members of both royal families were in attendance, with the exception of Oliza, and Salem's still missing mother. Danica Shardae and Zane Cobriana were standing just in front of the dais; Oliza's mother would still be queen of the avians after this night, but her father would have to relinquish his title. Nacola, once queen, and Sive Shardae, future heir to the avian throne, stood beside them. There was no need for the avian royal house to witness the serpiente succession, but their presence clearly showed

Shardae support for the Cobriana and hope for the continued alliance of Wyvern's Court.

I made my way down to the market square but refrained from approaching the royal family. They made no effort to seek me out. When Sive noticed me in the crowd, she smiled politely but edged closer to her alistair.

"Milady," Arqueete called out just then. The serpiente normally sold pastries in the early morning, but she was doing a brisk business in the ever growing crowd. "You haven't eaten today, have you?" she asked, looking me over.

When *had* I last eaten?

"It has been a while," I admitted.

"You need to take better care of yourself," she said. "I set aside some of those honey cakes I know you fancy, in case you came by. The dancer's nest is giving Salem and his mate an ornate formal ceremony, and it won't start until full dark. You have a few minutes yet to fortify yourself."

"The wolves are here," I observed, trying to distract the well-meaning but aggressive merchant. My appetite would return eventually, when the magic had calmed. Until then, trying to force food down my gullet would only bring it back up again.

"I know Kalisa Vahamil, but not the other one," Arqueete replied. "Are they mates?"

"Frektane and Vahamil are enemies," I said, already turning my attention to the white-haired man at the very edge of the market. The Obsidian guild had sent representatives here, too. Though they refused to be ruled by the Cobriana, the guild had not survived for as long as they had by being disinterested. They would know about everything that occurred that night.

As true dusk fell, dancers clad in elaborate silver and black *melos,* the traditional colors of the Cobriana royal house, went about lighting torches, until the market was as bright as at noontime. When finally the prince emerged with his queen-to-be, Rosalind, the image took my breath away. The next Diente and Naga made a beautiful pair. A ripple of appreciation ran through the crowd.

Then the peaceful moment was broken. Rosalind began to weep. And Salem—

No. That wasn't now. Salem was fine. Would be fine.

Had to be fine.

I was less interested in the elaborate ceremony than I was in the reactions of those watching it. Most serpents were enraptured by the royal pair, but more than a few exchanged concerned or outright skeptical glances. Were some of them beyond worried? Which ones might have treason on their minds?

Despite my cynical thoughts and the anxiety in the audience, when Salem kissed his mate, a tender sigh passed through the crowd. Couples among the serpiente moved closer together. Zane and Danica leaned against each other. I even saw Sive tentatively reach a hand toward her reserved alistair, though when her fingers brushed Prentice's, he looked startled and uncomfortable. She blushed and withdrew the attempted contact.

My eyes sought Nicias. He had positioned himself higher on the hills so he could see everything going on, and I was startled to find him looking toward me. He offered a tired half smile, and then his gaze moved on, scanning the crowd the same way mine had been.

I turned, and—

The door opened and Nicias entered, his face nearly gray with exhaustion.

"Oh, fates . . . what has happened?" Oliza gasped, pulling away from Betia as she saw the pained expression of her former guard and always friend.

I shuddered, pulling back from the vision at first—and then intentionally trying to move toward it. I needed to see what caused this future.

Oliza stumbled back, caught by her mate. "No," she whispered.

"Sive and Danica are working to keep . . ." Nicias looked away. "Oliza . . . they need you."

Her eyes brimmed with tears as she realized the consequences of this horror. "I . . . I will speak to . . ." She turned to kiss Betia goodbye, her voice choked up as she whispered, "My love."

And then there was only fire.

I was startled back from the vision when someone in the real world came to my side.

"It seems like you would have learned by now to be careful," I said as Vere Obsidian touched my arm. He was dressed as the dancers were, also wearing a black cloak embroidered with silver, which hid his white-viper features from the casual eye.

"I am always careful," he replied, "but being careful sometimes involves taking risks. I can see in your eyes when you start to drift away, and I can feel your magic waver when you are upset. What horrors do you see when you look at the new king?"

"Is Salem king already?"

The white viper nodded. "You must have lost quite a bit of time there. What was it you were seeing instead?"

"Why does it matter to you?"

He seemed to consider my words carefully. "Throughout history, the Cobriana have alternated between offering my people an olive branch and offering them a noose. I don't know this cobra. It worries me that when you look at him I can almost smell the blood."

"It isn't yours," I said.

"You've seen his reign?"

I shook my head. I had seen Oliza's reign, even though it had always ended in ice or fire. I had seen Sive's reign. The cobra had just been crowned king, and still, I could not see him rule.

"You mean for once the future is as much a mystery to you as to us mere mortals?" Vere joked.

"I—" Salem and his mate were moving toward us, through the crowd. "Do you care to introduce yourself to the current monarchy?"

The white viper hesitated for just a moment but then shook his head. "Not just yet. Take care of yourself, Hai." He squeezed my shoulder but was gone from my side before the Diente and his queen reached me.

"Hai, thank you for attending," Salem said, with what looked like a genuine smile.

The warm regard from the cobra unnerved me. I could only nod. "It seemed appropriate."

"Have you been introduced to Rosalind?"

"No, we haven't—" Halfway through offering my hand, I recoiled. For just a moment, I could almost taste the viper's tears. "I'm sorry. I . . ."

The dancer-queen, instead of looking insulted, looked relieved not to have to shake my hand.

Salem frowned. "Are you all right?"

Fortunately, before I had to answer, Sive found us in the crowd. "I'm sorry to interrupt," she said, touching Salem's wrist. "I was hoping I could get some advice." The hawk dropped her gaze, her expression more carefully controlled than she usually kept it around serpents.

"It's fine," I said, half curtsying, a habit from another world, as I excused myself.

Salem and Rosalind shrugged before turning their attention to Sive. I would always be a falcon to them. They didn't trouble themselves to worry about me.

CHAPTER 10

I retreated to the hills where Nicias sat, his attention on the celebration.

"Are you all right?" Nicias asked as I sat beside him. "I saw you talking to Salem and Rosalind. You looked upset."

"Did I?" I asked. I couldn't remember the last time I had *looked* upset, even when I had felt it. I glanced back at the celebration now, where Rosalind was dancing with one of her nestmates, and Salem and Sive were having what appeared to be an intense conversation. Salem leaned close to whisper something to her, and she blushed so deeply I could see her cheeks redden from where we were.

At the same moment, Nicias exclaimed, "You're hurt!"

I tried to hide my hand from him, but he caught my wrist. "It's nothing; I cut myself." I could not lie to him, *would* not, and so I did not want him to ask about it.

"I can tell that." His voice sounded distant. "It looks like it stopped bleeding a while ago. The lines are almost gone. What happened, Hai?"

"I would rather not answer that," I said, more curtly than I meant to.

Nicias closed his eyes for a moment, taking a deep breath before he answered, "I won't force you to." Still, he did not release my hand. I could feel the soft hum of his magic like a summer breeze. It sent a shiver through me that had nothing to do with the weather.

"Salem," I began. "It was—stupid," I said, changing my mind about telling Nicias what had happened in Gren's house. None of those falcons would harm Salem, knowing what I would do. My gaze returned to the new serpiente king, who was dancing with his mate. Sive seemed to be trying to cajole Prentice into doing the same.

"I see the way you look at him," Nicias said. "I assumed he was related to your recent distress. I don't have nearly your control over *sakkri*, but I can almost see your visions when I reach for you," he said. "They troubled me enough that I spoke to Salem. I would like to assign extra guards to him, but he is very much a cobra. He is confident in his followers' loyalty and, like most of his line, believes a show of force will only breed trouble." He sighed heavily. "And, if I understand *sakkri*, it is entirely possible that he is correct and will be perfectly safe until we overreact and put him in danger. Unless you have seen any details . . ."

I shook my head, my eyes still on the crowd. "I have seen his death, but that is all I see, not what leads to it." Normally I would say that Nicias was right. Many futures that had been nearly impossible happened purely because of meddling that would not have occurred if there had been no prophecy. This, though, felt stronger. Softly, I added, "I've never considered myself loyal to the Cobriana, but I am not a traitor to them, either. If I knew how to protect him, I . . ." All my attention suddenly turned to Sive Shardae, who had just given up on trying to get Prentice to dance and wrapped her arms around his neck and kissed him.

"Hai?"

I turned back to Nicias, intending to reassure him that my moment of distraction had nothing to do with insincerity when a shout pierced the air.

"Then leave me alone!"

Nicias sprang to his feet, searching the crowd for the source, which I had already located. Sive had just shoved Prentice away and was glaring at him. Before I could try to convince Nicias that our presence wasn't needed at a lovers' quarrel, he started hurrying toward the argument. I followed, though it quickly became obvious even to Nicias that the cry had been born more of frustration than of fear.

Prentice moved after his pair bond, protesting. "Sive, please, I didn't mean—"

"Didn't mean *what*?" Sive demanded. "To insult me, slander me, and my family, and my loved ones, all at the same time?"

Prentice cringed. "I spoke poorly. You know that's not—"

"Maybe it isn't what you meant to *say*, but it is what you *meant*," she argued. "Or maybe you would like to give some more specific details about how I'm acting 'like a dancer'?"

"Can we please discuss this somewhere else?" he begged, stepping toward her and dropping his voice—as if it would matter when everyone around them had gone dead silent. It wasn't every day that one had a chance to see a hawk in hysterics.

"Somewhere else?" Sive cooed. "Somewhere *private*? Are

you sure it would be seemly for us to be alone together—especially given all the lewd serpiente *habits* I seem to have picked up? People might *talk*."

I had seen criminals in front of the Empress's mercy, yet in all my life, I had never seen a man's face turn so gray.

"That . . . isn't . . ."

Salem finally stepped forward. He touched his cousin's arm, making her jump. "I'm sorry; this is my fault. Sive asked me—"

"*Your* fault?" Prentice growled, his voice dropping. "I suggest you stay out of this, snake. You've had your hands all over her all night, and I've had to stand by and listen to people tell me that's 'just how serpents behave.' Maybe it's—"

"Sive isn't a child!" Salem shouted. "She is a woman, and she knows what she wants, so maybe—oh, never mind." He shook his head. "Sive, I'm sorry."

"Go away, Prentice," Sive whispered. "Please, just . . . just go away."

The raven hesitated, and anyone could see true anguish in his expression. Finally Prentice bowed his head. "As milady wishes."

He changed form and disappeared into the sky. Sive turned and leaned against Salem for a moment.

"Let's get you somewhere private," Salem said softly. Then he turned to the crowd with a fiery glare, daring the nearest fool to look him in the eye. "There's nothing to see. *Go*. There's nothing worth watching here. Leave her alone." Serpents turned away, not eager to incur the wrath of their new king by harassing the distraught hawk.

Nicias and I did as Salem wished, too, walking away from

the chaos. This was a private matter, not one for guards, and clearly not one for me.

"What was that about?" Nicias asked.

"I suspect it was about Sive trying very hard to catch some less-than-brotherly attention from her alistair," I said, recalling the moment earlier when Sive had reached for Prentice's hand. "Perhaps following advice she had received from Salem."

Nicias arched an eyebrow. "Considering the outrageous behavior serpiente consider casual, friendly contact, I'm certain I don't want to know what advice a serpiente dancer would give a woman regarding how to entice her mate."

"What advice would you have given her?" I wondered aloud.

Nicias, avian-raised gentleman that he was, blushed. "That's not the kind of conversation I am likely to have with the heir to the Tuuli Thea."

"Which is probably why Sive went to a serpent. What avian would have answered her question?"

Nicias jumped, and only then did I realize that I had been reaching for him. "I'm going to try to speak to Salem about security again, if I can get a private moment with him," he said, obviously trying to change the topic. "You should rest, if you can. I know how tired you are."

When Nicias said he knew, he meant it. He must have felt my weakness the moment he had touched my hand earlier.

Instead of pulling back, I moved closer, made brazen by his concern and the passion of serpents still celebrating in the marketplace. I brushed my lips over his soft skin. "Come with me?"

Nicias hesitated, then shook his head. "I have—"

"A duty, I know," I said. "I will still be here when you've done it."

He put his hands on my shoulders, using just enough force to put me back at arm's length. "If I really thought you wanted companionship, I would give it to you," he said softly. "If I thought that you felt any form of desire for me, even if that was all, I would consider staying. But I've seen the way you go to men like Opal to hide from your pain. I've seen the way you treat him, and the way you let him treat you. I won't be another man you use to help you find oblivion. I'm sorry."

I crumpled as he turned away, and dropped my head in my hands.

It isn't like that with you, I argued. *It was never like that with you . . . if only you would listen, if only you would see . . .* But Nicias had blocked me from his mind and did not hear my pleas.

I collapsed on the soft grass of the northern hills and watched him go to the new Diente's side. Nicias and Salem spoke at length, and then Salem's Naga pulled Nicias into the crowd, entreating him to dance.

I closed my eyes.

Nicias had a duty. It would be easier to turn the Mercy from the Empress than it would be to turn Nicias from his damned *duty.*

CHAPTER 11

After Nicias left, I lay on the cool grass and closed my eyes, listening to the celebration from afar. Despite the serpents' swirled, half-formed magic, my mind remained oddly free of the violent visions that had plagued me for the past forty-eight hours.

Whatever was to be done, I knew, was done. One way or another, the decision that would either accept Salem as king or kill him had been made, and now I could hear the serpiente celebrating. Rosalind and her mate had withdrawn to a secluded den, but the king's people danced until dawn, when avian merchants began to emerge from their homes, determined not to be chased away by serpent festivities.

Perhaps, I thought, the world had shifted enough that this cobra was once again guarded by Ahnleh's grace. Maybe my conversation with Nicias, and his with Salem, had been enough to save him. That hope almost made me forget what a fool I'd been with Nicias and the way he had looked walking away from me.

Hope finally brought with it hunger. Ravenous, I descended into the market. There I found Arqueete, who was far too happy to give me breakfast when I admitted to my appetite.

"She looked so pale, though, when she left," I heard an avian man say as he passed me.

The person he had been speaking to answered, "It just doesn't seem . . ."

The conversation drifted out of my hearing range, but the merchant filled me in on their gossip. "Sive stayed for much of the celebration last night," Arqueete explained. "Apparently she looked upset when she went home."

I could imagine she had, after the fight with Prentice.

"She is all right, I assume?" I asked, vaguely aware that a couple of avian women were standing near us, listening.

Arqueete shrugged. "I haven't seen her since last night. She was pale, a little shaky, but she seemed to have calmed down from that argument."

Pale and shaky, a hawk? The serpent described her condition in an unconcerned tone, but anyone who had spent time with avians knew how much it took for them to become visibly upset. Then again, it took a lot to make one start screaming in the marketplace, too.

Another serpent, the flautist Salokin, approached the stall, drawn by our conversation. "I understand Sive's being upset. She just about threw herself at Prentice—an action I applaud, though her taste is questionable—and his response was less than enthusiastic. You should have heard what he said to her!" Salokin shook his head. "She'll be fine, though. A pretty girl like that isn't going to have any trouble finding someone else."

"True," the merchant answered. "Though, as for her *taste* . . ." She smirked. "Nah."

The avian women nearby were discussing the event, too, and I moved slightly toward them to hear better. "I just hope no serpent took liberties with her," one said. "I mean, she *is* still young, and very innocent, and even I know that serpiente have very different ideas of what's appropriate. I just hope no one took advantage of her."

"I think it would be good for her," Salokin commented, apparently also having eavesdropped on the women's conversation. "She's not ten; she's sixteen. A little fling never did a pretty girl harm."

Scandalized, the avian woman returned, "It does plenty of harm, especially when a lady has a very valiant alistair!"

"Valiant? Prentice?" another serpent scoffed. "On the most romantic night of the year, she has the audacity to try to *kiss* her *mate*—oh, the scandal!—and he puts her down like a child and tells her she's acting 'like a common serpiente whore.' "

"He did not!" one of the avians exclaimed.

"Oh, I'm sure those weren't his exact words," Arqueete interjected. "Even if the bird *knew* words like that, he would sooner die than speak them around a lady. Though that was pretty much the gist of it."

"You missed their earlier argument about Salem," Salokin said. "The Diente had just sworn to his mate, and Prentice was standing there telling Sive to stop flirting with her *cousin*."

"Only by marriage," Arqueete added under her breath.

"You have to admit, they do flirt," one of the avian ladies

said softly. "If she was my daughter, I would have called her to task over it."

"He's a serpent, and a dancer," one of the other avians said proudly, with her head held high. "Everyone knows that their form of friendly is simply forward. It doesn't mean anything."

As one of the two avian women cried, "Impossible!" I realized we had gathered quite a crowd.

"Stop this, stop it," another serpent said, breaking into the conversation. "Salem might not mind dancers gossiping about his affairs, but obviously Sive has been discreet on her side of the court."

Arqueete wasn't quite ready to change the subject. Speculating, she said, not nearly softly enough, "No wonder the hawk was feeling desperate—Salem's a mated man now."

"*Drop it,*" the third serpent snapped as one of the avian women gasped at the implication. "*He* has a mate and *she* has an alistair, and I'm sure neither Rosalind nor Prentice wants to know that Sive and Salem were together last night for some kind of . . ." He looked up and, realizing his words were reaching more people than he had intended them to, fell silent.

Worried, I looked at the surrounding faces, but even those who looked shocked also appeared slightly amused. There must have been enough serpiente influence on the avians of Wyvern's Court that they could feel scandalized without calling for blood. How progressive; Oliza would have been thrilled.

Then Salokin seemed to recall how the conversation had begun. "A woman isn't usually that upset after spending hours with her lover, and if she *was* involved with Salem, a little insult from a flustered raven like Prentice isn't likely to ruin her night."

Salokin's words caused an instant reaction, especially from the half dozen serpents who had come to Arqueete's stall now that the afternoon had begun.

"I hope you aren't implying—"

"I'm not implying anything," Salokin squeaked.

One of the avian women cleared her throat. "I think the discussion is over."

"I think someone should tell Prentice," the other avian woman remarked. "He'll forgive her, naturally."

"I'm sure he already knows," the first woman said.

My blood ran cold then, as suddenly I understood.

Nicias! I called out to him with all my magic and felt him respond.

I was immersed in another vision—only this time I knew I was witnessing the present, not some uncertain future.

Prentice was furious. He had seen how pale his pair bond had looked when she'd finally returned home from Salem's coronation. She had refused to continue their earlier argument and had claimed that her pallor was from fatigue, that she had hardly slept since Oliza had made the announcement and the late-night festivities had been too much for her.

Then, the next morning, he had heard the rumors.

His heart was pounding with rage, but his face was composed as he stepped past the guards who were watching the serpent's door.

"I need to speak to Salem," he said.

Prentice sounded calm, and they knew he was Sive's alistair. They probably assumed he was carrying some message from her. One of them knocked on Salem's door.

The cobra was still sleeping, probably in the arms of his mate, but Prentice insisted that it was an emergency—that he needed to speak to Salem quickly, before it got later.

"What is going on here?" Nicias demanded, in my real world.

I gasped, trying to move toward him. He had obviously landed just outside the crowd, which had become nastier in the moments I had been away from it.

"Nicias! You're one of Salem's guards now; you should deal with this," a serpiente merchant pleaded. "Sive was upset last night. Everyone knows that Salem has been flirting with her for months. They were alone together for part of last night—and this . . ." He spat a curse. "This pathetic excuse for a serpent dared suggest your king might have . . ." He struggled for words. "That she . . ."

"She was too upset to have spent those hours enjoying herself," someone said, an anonymous voice in a venomous crowd.

"Nicias," I shouted, trying to draw his attention to me.

"I need to speak to you alone," Prentice insisted when Salem came to the door. "Without your Naga, please?"

Salem frowned, noticing the chill in Prentice's voice and assuming something was wrong. "Yes, of course. Rosalind, would you mind giving us a moment?"

The woman, who looked as if she had tugged on clothing as Prentice had waited at the door, gave Salem a playful smile. "I suppose." She kissed her mate on the cheek as she left. "I'll meet you in the nest, whenever you're free."

82

Nicias's voice was cold as he demanded, "You're a serpent. Of all people, you know how serious a crime you are accusing Salem of. What proof do you have?"

"What proof do we need?" Salokin replied. "I saw the look on her face—"

"*I* saw no distress, only fatigue," Nicias said. "I heard her tell her alistair she was fine when she met back up with him. I saw nothing that would found this foul a rumor."

"Salem's a cobra," someone else said softly. "You're one of his guards. Of course you're going to be loyal to him."

"I'm loyal enough not to accuse the Diente, who last night was beyond any suspicion, of raping the heir to the Tuuli Thea."

"Nicias!" I shouted, and this time he turned to me. "They don't matter," I said quickly. "Prentice has already heard. He—"

Nicias had shifted shape and torn into the skies before I could explain that Salem was no longer in his room and Prentice was no longer in his; both were in a secluded spot.

Shoving people out of my way, I raced up the hills, my lungs burning and my heart longing for wings. I stumbled at the edge of the forest as Prentice drew his blade.

Salem dodged the first attack, shouting, "What is—" He rolled to avoid another attack. I could tell he didn't want to engage in the fight because he didn't want to harm his opponent.

I reached their side and struggled against visions as I dove at Prentice, bearing him to the ground. Again I shouted to Nicias, telling him where we were, and felt him back in the air, diving.

I threw Prentice away with strength I should not have had and ran to Salem's side. I had arrived in time to stop Prentice from landing a lethal blow, but there was a scratch across Salem's forearm that was already turning purple-black.

"No!"

Avian guards no longer used poison regularly, but Prentice had access to it. He had known he was up against a cobra.

Nicias landed and caught Prentice's wrists, but I was only barely aware. *A'she, she*—future, present—were blurring, blending, contorting and twisting—

Salem Cobriana lay in my arms, dying. His body was cold; his red eyes had turned a tawny brown; his heartbeat raced, pushing the poison faster, deeper, while his lungs fought paralysis. I could barely feel *him*, his life, anymore. Slipping away.

I knew I could save him; I had that power, always had. I could use my magic to heal the tissues and destroy the poison . . . but terror gripped me. I could ask the magic for that much, and she would grant the favor, but she would ask more than I wanted to give in return. I could swim her dark, still waters, but what if I drowned?

"Nicias!" I shrieked, even though I knew what the result would be. He had taken the time to immobilize Prentice, to guard our backs, and now it was too late for him to make any difference.

I covered Salem with my body, wishing I could give him my warmth, but did not reach out to him with the greedy magic that could save his life. I *couldn't*. Please . . .

I had fought so hard to stay in this world. Calling on my magic now could mean giving it all up and returning to the void darkness, where I would not even remember why I had fought at all.

Nicias reached his fallen monarch's side. He did what I would not, reaching out with his magic, but the attempt was clumsy. He had no training. . . .

No.

Not this time.

I knew where Salem's death led, and it was a darker path than Ecl.

I felt his life slip away, and I grabbed at it. He was trying to follow Brysh into the darkness of death. I bid goodbye to Wyvern's Court, and I dove after him.

CHAPTER 12

*L*eben appeared to the Dasi, and they knelt in misguided worship.

Maeve leaned against the creature, whispering in his ear with a smile, as Kiesha watched from the lonely darkness. The priestess of Anhamirak hid her tears.

Maeve wept as she was wrapped in the arms of the Nesera'rsh. She had done what she needed to protect her people, but she had lost . . . everything. Everything that mattered to her.

Without her, the balance ruptured, and the Dasi began to crumble.

Cjarsa, falcon priestess of Ahnmik, watched the first of her disciples fall to Ecl. Leben had given them wings, and he had given them madness. One was not worth the other.

This had to be stopped.

Kiesha shrieked as magic that should have called rain for the crops brought lightning and deluge. She cradled a drowned infant in her arms. Her people were dying, and everything she did to try to help them only made it worse.

Araceli and Brassal, the priest of Namid, *struggled; Araceli's daughter was caught in the middle, and at the end she was limp and cold. Brassal backed out of the room with his hands held in front of him; he stared at them as if they were alien growths instead of his own flesh.*

The Dasi's altars were scorched, frozen, shattered—only ruin left behind—and their priests and priestesses struggled against the magic that cut their bodies and souls.

They cursed Maeve, who had enticed Leben into giving them these "gifts," the magic of their second forms. When people began to die, the new serpents blamed the falcons—those who worshipped death, sacrificed to it.

Magic and blades and fire and blood . . . so much blood, soaking the red sand.

"You say you wish to end this," Kiesha said, greeting the falcons.

"Before more lives are lost," Araceli said.

The hawk child Alasdair screamed as half of Kiesha's magic was shoved into her, and that scream echoed for generations: two thousand years of slaughter between the avians and the serpiente,

*which the falcons manufactured in an attempt to avoid the deaths of
countless more.*

*Years later, the hawk child Danica screamed as Anjay tore his
knife into her alistair's heart. A falcon mother screamed as that cobra was killed by another one of Alasdair's descendents.*

*I screamed as magic ripped into me and tore my wings away,
and I fell from Ahnmik's skies.*

*Oliza screamed as the magic of her daughter, Keyi, destroyed
her; and Nicias screamed as he fought the Mercy who had come to
take Sive's daughter, Aleya, and Salem's son, Zenle, away–*
No!

That much I could stop.

The rest of these images were long gone, ash in the wind,
but Keyi was still the future, and the future could be
changed.

With one final shriek, I slammed into Salem's magic like
a blade into water, gasping and choking as I forced myself
deeper. The world swirled—violet, white, black, red. Dis-
tantly, I was aware that my body was somewhere.

I could hear my breath and my heartbeat slowing . . .
slowing . . .

The shards of Anhamirak's magic in Salem were searing,
and I felt them slice into my mind as I struggled to retain my
focus. The poison—

There was a black cobra at the edge of my field of vision,
but when I twisted to see, it was gone.

The poison. Falcons had created it; I needed to destroy it. I concentrated, and brought into view the places where Salem's undulating magic shuddered, the golden waves becoming black and charred.

The poison consisted of two parts. The primary ingredient was a toxin, which would cause little damage in the bodies of most shapeshifters; we healed too quickly for that.

However, there was a spell built into the poison, and I struggled to read it as it devoured even more of the magic that made Salem a serpent. The patterns kept shifting, melding themselves with the lines of that which they destroyed.

So vulnerable, I realized. The Cobriana had only half of the magic they had been created with; the other half had been used long before to form the avians. The falcons had cleverly fashioned the poison to meld with what remained of Anhamirak's power. Once it ate away at the magic that protected serpiente flesh, the base toxins could stop the heart and end the life.

I twisted about, wrapping that deadly magic around myself like spiderwebs. Strands ripped and shifted as I reached for them and altered the patterns to make the spell harmless.

I shoved the energy that made Salem's heart spasm into him. Again, again, again, until it beat on its own. I did the same for his lungs, making them rise and fall.

I surveyed the damage, and it was vast.

Left behind by the poison's onslaught was a battered, crippled remnant of the magic Salem should have had, *needed* to have. His body was performing the motions of life now, but his soul . . .

Was that lost?

I could force animation of Salem's body, but the poison had done so much damage that his mind and spirit had fled. I reached out as far as I could, trying to find him.

Again I saw a cobra at the edge of my vision, and I spun about, shouting, "Salem!"

Suddenly I slipped on a patch of black ice. On all fours, I scurried back as the ice began to crumble. Where—*Salem!* I screamed, but received no response.

Nothing.

Except a voice, an echo of the darkness I had once loved, whispering, *You have tried and failed, my love, my sweet. You have done all you can do, so rest now. Sweet failure grants no future decisions. It is over; let it be over.*

Ecl.

An icy breeze swirled through the illusion, and the skies darkened. Before me I could see a black castle, its dark and cold spires rising. Slipping, scrambling, I moved away from it, still reaching out with my magic. . . . I couldn't find anyone, anything, not even Nicias.

I had often wanted to return here since he had pulled me away, but I *couldn't*, not now.

Why, my sweet? They do not need you. You have done all you can do and it was not enough. Rest.

I crumbled, feeling the world go cold as the walls of my ancient black palace grew around me. I slammed my fists against them, and for a moment they rang like bells. Images of Wyvern's Court flashed in the darkness.

People rioting and shouting. The serpiente screaming for blood, avians demanding justice, rumors rife, hatred stirred. I recoiled without meaning to.

Then the sounds faded. Again I struck the black walls, but this time there was silence.

A falcon circled overhead, flickering into and out of the blackness of the sky.

I watched a woman cross the ice down below, her footsteps fatigued. She knelt by the gates. I tried to scream her name, but this land could hold no sound.

Mother, I shrieked, but Darien heard nothing.

She left behind pink roses, tucked into the chains that barred the door. Dimly I recalled that she had been here before; we both had been. This was an illusion formed of something less than memory—an echo of what once might have been.

Beasts prowled the land outside, ripping themselves out of the ice when threatened and then fading back into the void when my attention wandered. They were attracted by Anhamirak's warmth and held at bay only by my falcon magic. If I struggled, they returned, drawn like sharks to blood.

Soon even they faded away, and there was nothing. Then *I* ceased to be.

Ka'hena'she.

We are not.

Ka'hena'o'she-ka'hena'a'she.

We never were; we never will be. We return to the void we never left, for *Mehay* is the center of all, and all is the center of nothing.

Somewhere deep in that center, I glimpsed something quiet, a gentle vision of the world that still existed . . . somewhere.

Sive was leaning against a post and trying very hard not to tremble. She was the heir to the avian throne now; she wasn't supposed to lose control this way.

Salem and Prentice, both gone. How could they both be gone?

She had told the guards to take Prentice away. Now she had to strike from her mind the sound of his pleas, his begging her to understand that he had only been trying to protect her. Begging her to forgive him. Begging her not to let them execute him.

"Please, Shardae."

Sky above, take the echo of those words from her brain. Take away the image of him kneeling before her, his hands bound and tears on his face, and let her rest.

Someone walked up behind her and she tensed, wondering if the fiend who had plotted Salem's death by planting those vile rumors had made plans for hers as well. She was alone here; that was why she had come here instead of returning to the Rookery after she had addressed her people.

Silently, the stranger put his arms around her, holding her gently against him, as unimposing as he could be while still offering support. Suddenly Sive Shardae, heir to the Tuuli Thea, did something she had never done before.

She turned around, leaned against him, and began to cry.

Part of her was vaguely aware that he was a serpent, maybe a dancer, probably one of the many people who had loved and respected Salem Cobriana. But not, thank the gods, one of the many who blamed her for their king's death.

Tears fell silently from Sive's eyes as she let him hold her, as she listened to his heartbeat and matched her breathing to his and tried to think nothing.

CHAPTER 13

To another, it might have been a tragic moment. To me, it held a quiet beauty. I struggled to see more, desperate to remember the gentle compassion and the way it had moved me, and again the ice trembled, this time allowing someone else's magic to slip through.

Hai.

A thought returned to my drifting mind, that single word: *Hai.* Vaguely, I remembered . . . that was me. . . .

Hai!

I thrashed as if in a drugged sleep, and again images pressed upon my mind. *Salem, poison, pain*—no, I didn't want that. *Sive, and a friendly stranger holding her.* Gentleness.

Someone was calling to me, and I could not help looking as outside my black palace the beasts groggily pulled themselves to the surface, hissing and snarling at an invader who sullied the darkness.

Echoes of what had been.

A panther leapt, drawing blood from the invader foolish enough to try to walk here. The crimson stain made the ice resonate, and I squeezed my eyes shut and crumpled into a ball, trying to block out the pain.

I had been here before.

"I won't leave you here!" the man shouted, but his voice was fading.

Serpents coiled around him, choking away the breath that with every exhalation made the ice near him steam.

I moved to the gates of my tower but was blocked by jagged ice before I could reach the interloper. He lifted his eyes to me, and they were as blue as opals. Nicias's tears fell and the tower fractured allowing me another step.

"Daughter of *shm'Ahnmik'la'Darien'jaes'oisna'ona'saniet' mana'heah'shm'Ecl* and Anjay Cobriana," he said. "Beautiful dancer Hai." I felt the words wrap around me as tightly as chains, and I moved forward once again.

The serpents shuddered and moved away from Nicias, their bodies contorting as if burned by his blood, red on their black scales. The panther continued to snarl, the sound a silent vibration through the ice. Finally I knelt beside Nicias, and he lifted a hand to touch my cheek.

"You cannot stay here," he told me. "I will not let you."

Cold.

I had never felt cold from him before, but the ice seemed to be seeping into Nicias as his blood flowed out. Too late, probably. At this point, it would be far easier to consign him to the void and follow him down.

Rest with me, someone whispered. My own voice, stolen by the darkness.

"Rest," Nicias echoed. He tried to shake his head and trembled.

Sive and her silent savior weren't the only ones comforting each other. I tried to draw on the compassion I could feel beneath the fury in Wyvern's Court, but blood was the only color in this land, the only heat, and it was feeding the creatures. They paced closer.

What have I done?

I had chosen this exile from reality; I had sought it, to escape the pain of my failures. I was meant to be here, but *he* was not. Nicias was light, and warmth, not this blackness. I held him against me as the monsters paced around us, and I felt the world quiver.

It would be easier to let him fall.

The knowledge tempted me too much.

"Nicias," I whispered. I kissed his forehead, trying to gather his warmth when everything around us was trying to take it away. "Nicias, my light. Please."

I shrieked into the darkness: *"You cannot have him!"* My voice faded into nothingness without so much as an echo.

The panther snarled, and I wanted desperately to scramble back into the palace to hide, but I couldn't give up on Nicias. If I fell now, Nicias would fall with me. I knew he would rather be dead than consigned to this void world.

"Please, Nicias," I prayed. "You're the only one who knows the way out of here. *Please . . .*"

I felt a sliver of awareness from him and tried to pull on it, dragging us both gruelingly across the sharp ice. Somehow, painfully, I found my way back to the *she.*

And then we were on a familiar bed—Nicias's, in his home in Wyvern's Court. My hands were gripping his so tightly I did not wonder why no one had separated us.

His skin writhed with my tarnished magic. Strips of power had lashed his arms, face, chest and back. His lungs barely moved and his heart barely beat, but I could fix that.

I gasped, my body going into spasms and my back arching in pain, as I lured the first loop of cutting magic away from him the only way I knew how. My magic preferred its owner. It cut into my body instead of his.

Another loop, and this time I cried out, feeling the skin on my back split. Blood seeped into my clothing. Another line, another slice, another shriek. How many times would I accidentally kill this peregrine?

Nicias stirred, drawing a breath as I removed the bands around his throat. His eyes opened. They held a dazed, lost look that nevertheless was one of the sweetest sights I had ever seen.

Exhausted, I wrapped my arms around Nicias's neck and laid my cheek against his shoulder, breathing deeply and trying to memorize his scent. My body was shaking from the pain it had absorbed and the effort of pulling us both back into this world, but the ache faded as Nicias took over the healing process.

"I couldn't leave you there," I whispered. "Why did you . . . why did you come for me?"

"I couldn't leave *you* there," he said.

Hungrily, I lifted my face to his, tasting his lips. Instead of the ashes of nothingness I had found with others, Nicias had a spark that drew me *here* and *now*. After a moment of surprise, he returned my kiss, his lips even softer than the feathers I felt at the nape of his neck.

I combed his hair back from his face with my fingers, savoring the silky texture.

He started to pull away, and I clung to him desperately.

"Please," I said. "Nicias, you drew me back from the Ecl and gave me the world. If you asked me to dance, I feel like I could fly. How could you ever doubt what you mean to me?" I whispered, addressing his fears before he could speak them. There were tears in my eyes, which had been dry for many years. "Please," I whispered. "Believe me. I love you."

He caressed my cheek; I closed my eyes, leaning toward his hand. "I believe you," he said.

"Then stay."

When I opened my eyes, he was shaking his head. "Hai, I left Salem unconscious, possibly dying, to go after you. I can't stay longer, not without knowing how he is."

Salem.

After risking so much, and experiencing a kind of hell that only a falcon could ever truly know, how could I possibly have forgotten who we had done it for?

I needed to know what would happen next.

I smiled wryly, realizing that Cjarsa had been wrong about one thing. Apparently a mongrel *could* understand things such as loyalty and duty . . . at least well enough to let go of this beautiful peregrine and say, "You're right."

Nicias kissed my forehead, lingering a moment longer before we both pulled back, and rose to face the world that Fate had left to us.

I would never be able to replace Nicias's love for his wyvern Oliza or supplant his responsibility to his Diente, Salem. But for now it was enough, for me, to see the reluctance in his movements as we stepped out his front door and into the bustle of the marketplace.

"I think I heard the doctor say she was taking Salem back to his room in the Rookery," Nicias said, leading the way to Wyvern's Court's royal keep.

When we reached the Rookery and ascended the stairs to the top floor, we found guards in front of Salem's door.

They nodded to Nicias in respectful greeting and said to us, "Sive Shardae is inside."

Nicias had just lifted his hand to knock when the door opened, revealing the young hawk, who did not manage to keep the sorrow and fatigue from her face.

"Nicias, Hai," she said. Her voice was still musical and calm, but exhaustion had given it a rough edge, and she didn't quite focus on us when she spoke. "We found you with Salem—" She drew a breath, trying to compose herself, and then said, "It is good to see you well."

"Thank you," Nicias answered her. "Has he woken yet?"

Sive shook her head. "Not yet, and the doctors do not know if he will. They say that by all rights he should be dead. The poison . . ." Her voice dropped, but resolutely she continued, "Prentice used the strongest poison he could get his hands on."

We knew it all too well. Neither of us had the courage to ask the next reasonable question, but Sive must have known what we were wondering.

"Prentice has officially been exiled from my people," she said, "and given over to the serpiente to face judgment. If

Salem survives, he will be the one to judge his attacker. If he dies, Prentice will be executed, in accordance with nest law."

She looked back at the door she had just come through, as if willing the cobra on the other side to wake.

"Oliza has returned," Sive added. "She is Salem's heir, and if he dies, she will need to take the serpiente throne."

Sive's gaze drifted out the window. On the ground below, I saw the image of a now familiar figure.

Keyi darted among merchants, running into this one and that one as she evaded her mother, Oliza. The child was laughing as Oliza shook her head, smiling fondly.

Vere Obsidian sneaked through the crowd and took his daughter by surprise, lifting her around the waist.

I reached for Nicias's hand, needing contact, comfort, *anything*, because in that moment I wasn't numb. I could feel despair, and hopelessness, and shame.

I had seen Keyi time and again. I had seen Salem's death. The visions had unsettled me, and I had stirred myself to speak to the Empress and the falcons, but what had I *done* to prevent this from happening?

Until the moment when the cobra had been dying in my arms, I had done little more than hope for the best . . . and now we would all suffer the consequences of my naïveté and weakness.

I, who could see quite clearly all our futures, had no excuse for this failure. I should have done something differently.

Was it too late, or could I still?

Sive leaned against the wall, whispering, "Salem should be king. Oliza should be allowed to be with the woman she loves. Prentice should—" She broke off. "Once Salem named his mate, he secured the title for his generation, and the succession never goes backward while there is a legitimate heir. Besides, an infertile couple can't rule the serpiente, and Irene hasn't had any children in the last twenty years."

Sive was rambling. Everyone in the room knew it, but she didn't seem able to help her own words.

Finally her eyes focused, on us. "Please. Is there anything you can do for him? *Please*."

"We'll try," Nicias promised her.

She reached out and caught my hand. "Hai, I know you and I have never been close. Your prophecies—the idea that our destiny might not be of our own design, might be completely out of our hands, terrifies me. But if you can tell me . . . please, will he wake? Do you know? Do you know who started those horrible rumors, or if . . . Is this my fault?"

Nicias gently took her hand off mine. "None of this was your fault," he said.

"I should go," she said to us. "I have obligations. I have to . . ."

"It's all right." I was not good at giving comfort, but I could try. "You do what you must. I swear to you, we will do everything we can for Salem."

"Th-thank you. I'm sorry, I—I should go," she whispered again, as if that one decision was still too difficult.

"Someone should go with her," Nicias said to one of the other guards as Sive started to walk away alone.

I shook my head. "She'll be fine."

"You can't be sure of that," the guard said. He looked from Nicias to me.

Nicias turned to me. "Hai, you're certain?"

"Yes, I am." Sive would be queen; she always reigned in the futures I envisioned, except when Oliza's child killed us all. "For now she needs time to be alone. She can't grieve if someone else is there."

But she wouldn't be alone. I could see her already snuggling close to the serpent who had first comforted her. He held her quietly, because someone needed to.

"Then we'll let her be alone."

"Yes, sir," the guard replied before we moved forward to check on Salem.

We entered the sickroom with Sive's despair heavy in our hearts, and it only settled deeper when I saw the cobra.

Salem was pale and still. His heartbeat was slow but even, and his breath rose and fell, yet I sensed no life from him. Normally my magic reacted to Anhamirak's fiery power in Kiesha's kin, but in this case I felt nothing.

Salem's body had survived, but that was all.

He would not wake.

He would live until his body starved, but he would never again open his garnet eyes. I knew that as surely as I knew Ecl's damning darkness. And I knew that nothing good would become of this world without him.

Behind me, I heard Keyi cry.

CHAPTER 14

"No!" the child shouted.

Oliza frowned. "Keyi, you need to–"

"Don't wanna!" The child pouted and launched into a tantrum. "No, no, no!"

"Keyi, do I need to–"

Oliza cried out, recoiling from her daughter as golden red bands of magic whipped across her arms, drawing blood. Her eyes widened with sudden terror.

"Calm down, Keyi, please," she said.

Keyi continued to wail and stomp her feet, sending a stream of scalding magic at Oliza. Oliza screamed and fell, and only then did Keyi's tears stop.

"Mommy?"

Keyi hurried to Oliza's side, her eyes wide and afraid. "Mommy?" she wailed. "Mommy?" Her hands touched the blood as she shook Oliza, begging her to wake. "Mommy, come back! Mommy? Mommy, get up, please. I won't cry anymore. Mommy!"

"I need to talk to Oliza," Nicias was saying. "I—she—oh, gods."

"Nicias, you can't!" I cried, spinning toward him. "She can't rule. You know that."

He shook his head. "It isn't my decision."

"It needs to be someone's," I snapped. "You of all people know the possible consequences if Oliza returns to the throne."

"And *you* of all people know that Araceli's predictions are not to be trusted," he replied. "Darien believes it is possible to protect any children Oliza might have, and Cjarsa trusts Darien's judgment. Since Oliza is returning only as Diente, she won't need to worry about choosing a mate the avians will accept—"

"Nicias, don't be a fool." Instinctively, I reached toward him magically, trying to show him. If he could only see what I had seen—

Nicias recoiled, slamming magical walls between him and me so fast that I felt as if I had been slapped.

"Nicias, please, listen to me." I begged without shame, but I could see in his eyes that it was no use. I had been careless in my haste and had warmed the seeds of mistrust that still lingered in Nicias from his time on Ahnmik. He had experienced firsthand how powerfully manipulative a falcon's persuasion magics could be, and he would not allow himself to be fooled a second time.

What he might never understand was that there was no magic more powerful than that his own mind could use to convince itself that it was right.

"Nicias, I have seen the future in which Oliza takes the throne. I have seen you screaming when—"

"You have said yourself, many times, that *sakkri* can be misleading. They can show us that which we most fear." Before I could argue, he added, "You are not the only falcon who can spin a *sakkri*, Hai. Your mother has hope."

"My mother can't see past Oliza's magic."

"And Cjarsa?"

Was wrong. I didn't know how, but Cjarsa was *wrong*. Yes, *sakkri* could be misleading, but this one was too real. I believed absolutely that if Oliza took the throne, this world would be destroyed. Cjarsa feared the return of a wyvern so much that I could not understand how she could possibly be fooled by the hope that Nicias would be able to keep us all safe by binding the magic. How could she not *see*? Long before, it had taken all of the four falcons' power to tear Anhamirak's magic in half to keep it subdued. How could anyone believe that one prince, who had begun to study his magic only a few months earlier, could do what the high priestesses of Ahnmik and Brysh and the priest of Ecl could not?

"I will try to warn her of the danger, but, Hai, Oliza is all we have left," Nicias said. "If you are afraid of what might happen, then *help* us. Your magic is as powerful as mine. I know it overwhelms you sometimes, but despite that handicap, you still wield it with more precision and power than I can. I do believe we can protect Oliza. I would like to have you on our side."

I closed my eyes, letting a million futures drift before them. I saw Keyi. I saw fire, and I saw ice. I saw Rosalind weeping, Sive cold and dead, Nicias shrieking—

"I love you," I said, opening my eyes. "I have come to care

for Wyvern's Court, and for Oliza. I do not know what Cjarsa does or does not know, or what my mother does or does not believe." All I knew was that my mother would risk much to prove Araceli wrong and to get Nicias back on the island. "But I . . . I swear, I will do all I can to keep Wyvern's Court safe."

To Ahnmik, who holds all vows true, this I swear.

"Speak to Oliza," I said. "I will be here when you return."

Oliza already didn't trust me; if Nicias wouldn't believe me, there was no use arguing with the wyvern. She would trust her loyal guard over any other falcon. However, I had spoken true when I had made my promise to Nicias.

Because he was wrong.

Oliza *wasn't* all we had left.

I walked through Wyvern's Court with a deep weight in my heart.

Nicias, you gave me this pain, I thought, weeping. *If it wasn't for you, I would never have loved this land. I would never have needed to fight for it.*

I found myself at the green marble plaza, at the very center of Wyvern's Court, regarding the tall marble statue there. The wyvern looked so proud and sure.

I knelt and pressed one hand to the statue's base. From this spot, I could feel the heartbeat of the land.

I could also hear the argument Nicias was having with Oliza. Though I was glad that some of my warnings had reached him, I knew they would not be enough.

"I'm not returning as wyvern; I'm returning as Diente," Oliza said when Nicias pointed out, as I had, that there had been many reasons for her to leave the first time. "I need to fill only the one role, so there will be no conflict as long as I choose a serpent for my mate."

"And your child?" Nicias asked.

This, too, Oliza had an answer to. "The Dasi's magic became unbalanced when Maeve left the coven, but there is a group where that balance has been preserved among her descendents."

"Obsidian."

"Yes. I wouldn't have been able to make the alliance as wyvern, but as Diente, I can. Their leader is . . ." Oliza's voice wavered a little. She had no words of love to speak. "He is not a bad man. He has been kind to me."

I could already hear the child I had seen in the woods, Obsidian's wyvern child, laughing.

I closed my eyes and sent my spirit outward as I whispered a prayer to Ahnmik.

"White falcon, give me strength. Help me do what must be done."

"Obsidian will make a good Nag. He leads well and is charismatic enough that I think he will be able to earn the favor of our people despite the prejudice against white vipers."

"Your people will be uneasy enough about your choosing a new mate," Nicias warned. "And even if you weren't pledged already, you know that the serpiente won't react well to anything they see as *a political marriage. It is going to be difficult to force a white viper on them at the same time."*

"I don't have a choice!" Oliza snapped, *the words choked by sobs.* "Gods . . . Salem." *She bowed her head, no doubt struggling to compose herself, to stop thinking of her dying cousin and her abandoned love.*

Prying myself away from Oliza and Nicias, I turned my prayers to another deity.

"Anhamirak," I said, "you have never answered me. The magic of my mother's ancestors ripped your serpiente worshippers in half, and all I have to call you by are the shreds left behind. I know that. But please, I'm struggling for your people now. Please, if ever you would help a mongrel, make it now."

"It's the only option," *Oliza was saying.*

"It isn't a perfect solution, but . . . there might be some way you could adopt–"

Oliza shook her head. "If all I wanted was to be safe from my magic, that would be the answer–but if I must do this, make this choice, then I want more to show for it than survival. The Obsidian guild has been abused by the Cobriana for millennia. Anjay Cobriana promised them equality, but his death destroyed that chance. My father was pledged to a white viper, and then ended up executing her. I have a chance to make this right."

Oh, Oliza, there is no way to make this right.

"Ahnleh . . ."

What could a mortal say to the merciless Fate?

I forced myself to my feet.

A'le-Ahnleh was the traditional end to a prayer. By the will of Fate.

"*A'le-la,*" I whispered defiantly.

By *my* will.

I had plans to make.

When Nicias returned to Wyvern's Court, his steps were heavy with sorrow and exhaustion, and his beautiful eyes were distant.

"My love," I said, greeting him.

He leaned against me. "I spoke to Oliza. She will be here in the morning and will speak to her parents, and then she will make the announcement of her return in the evening."

I wrapped my arms around him. "It's all right," I said. "We will make it all right. But you should rest for now."

He took a deep breath and whispered, "Stay with me tonight?"

"Yes," I said, the word a prayer. "Tonight."

And then, the next day, I would lose him.

He lowered his head, and we kissed. It was sweet, and gentle, and it made tears come to my eyes.

"Just hold me," I said. "I love you. Please believe that. Please trust me. I love you. I have always loved you."

He kissed me again and then picked me up in his arms and carried me inside to his bed.

We wove between us the magic known by every lover—that powerful spell of passion. We slept side by side beneath soft blankets. We dreamed, accompanied by the music of our breath and heartbeats.

Peregrine and gyrfalcon wings, hair like sunlight tangled with strands the deep tone of a cobra's scales, skin like alabaster next to skin the color of honey, coated with a sheen of sweat. This was bliss.

The morning came too soon.

I dressed and then pulled open a drawer in the bedside table. Silently, I removed a small bundle, which Nicias had brought back from Ahnmik at the behest of my mother, and which had remained here in his home. I had not wanted it.

I still did not want it. Nevertheless, I unwrapped the hand-carved box in which my mother had kept all her mementos of my father. With shaking hands, I retrieved my father's signet ring. I stared at it for a long time before slipping it on.

"Please trust me," I whispered again to Nicias when it came time for us to part. *Don't hate me*, I silently begged his still-sleeping form, *for what I am about to do.*

CHAPTER 15

I looked back from the doorway, my heart pounding. Nicias looked so peaceful, lying there. Innocent. What I was about to do to him . . .

Suddenly he wasn't peaceful but once again screaming, fighting.

"How can you do this to me?" he shrieked at the falcon who was holding Zenle Cobriana. "All your high ideals, all your dreams—you are no better than your Empress!"

Darien looked away sadly as she cradled the cobra child.

All she said was "This cannot be allowed to happen again."

I shuddered. Nicias would probably never forgive me for what I was about to do, but *I* would never forgive myself if I didn't do it.

I saddled Najat and pounded into the woods with the word *traitor* echoing in my head.

At the edges of Obsidian land, I saw once again the child I had hoped I could banish.

Keyi twirled among the trees, chasing fireflies in the night air, while her father watched her fondly with pale green eyes.

Vere Obsidian loved his daughter more than life itself, and that showed on every inch of his face.

The white viper greeted me when I reached the camp, though he appeared distracted. "Hai, what brings you here so early in the day?"

Reasoning with Vere might get him to change his plans, but even if he backed out of his engagement to the wyvern princess, it did not mean she would change her mind.

"I came to offer my congratulations," I said instead. "I hear you are going to be king."

He looked away from me, toward the camp. "Apparently," he said.

"That's a bold move, for a man from a tribe that has sworn neither to lead nor to follow."

He nodded. "It is more than I would want, but Oliza's offer was . . ." He sighed. "This whole situation is appalling."

"Then why did you agree to it?"

"Oliza offered a pardon for all my people, without the

conditions her ancestors often tried to impose. They do not need to return to serpiente land or accept the Diente as king. She swore that the royal house would acknowledge the autonomy of the Nesera'rsh, as Maeve's coven once did, and that the Obsidian guild would be allowed to live as it wished, provided we break no serpiente laws."

"Do you love her?" I asked. As a rule, serpiente didn't believe in political marriage.

Vere shrugged. "I love my people."

"What of Betia?"

He winced. "I don't think I will ever be able to clear from my mind the expression on that woman's face when Nicias landed in front of Oliza. She knew what it meant before he said a word."

I'd learned enough. Now I had other visits to make.

"I will see you this evening, then."

"This evening."

My next visit was to the marketplace. It was still early, but I found Salokin speaking to Arqueete as she set out her wares for the day. They did not seem surprised to see me, and the way Arqueete dropped everything to give me her undivided attention the moment I approached told me where their loyalties lay.

The two serpents followed me, without question, to a less crowded area of the market.

"Salokin, you implied once that you might support me if I chose to assert my right as Anjay Cobriana's only child," I said, too softly for my voice to carry beyond these two. "If that is true, I need your vow on it."

His eyes widened as if I had asked him to sign his name

in blood. To a falcon, a spoken vow was much the same thing, though I did not think he knew that.

"I was loyal to your father," he answered firmly. "You are his child, his only heir. If you choose to step forward as Arami, then I swear I will be loyal to you."

Arqueete had put a hand on Salokin's arm to steady herself. She declared, "I served as a soldier beneath your father, before his death. I followed him to the Keep on the day he—" Her voice broke, but her fiery gaze remained on mine as she said, "I would have died in his place if I could have, and I would do the same for his heir. I swear it."

"I understand there are others?"

"Many others," Salokin answered immediately.

"When Oliza returns to Wyvern's Court to take the throne, I expect every serpent loyal to me to be in the crowd, at the front. Arqueete, if there are other trained soldiers in the group, I would appreciate their assistance. They are *not* to touch the princess. Make that very clear. They are simply to be there, in case I need them."

"Yes, milady."

I started to turn, then hesitated, looking back. "And, whoever is responsible for this . . . turn of events," I added, keeping all judgment clear from my voice, "I want them present. They should receive some recognition."

Salokin and Arqueete both nodded, deeply enough that they almost bowed. I did not know yet if they had started the rumors that had brought about Salem's demise, or just repeated them. Either way, I needed Salokin and Arqueete for a few hours more. It would be best to let them think I meant to reward them, until I was ready to act.

*   *   *

I returned then to the candle shop on the northern hills, where I found Opal, Gren, Maya and Spark in heated conversation. The instant I stepped into the room, the four falcons began to proclaim their innocence.

"Hush," I snapped. "Not one of you is stupid enough to have planned this against my will. I am not the Mercy, who would arrest you all for wanting it to be done even when you had no hand in it."

They all calmed, but I could see the wariness on their faces.

"You have all spoken of me as queen of this land, many times. Do you still wish it?"

Maya was the first to react. She knelt beside me, and I felt a chill go down my spine. I had seen others grovel this way before the Empress, but I was no royal falcon—only a mongrel, desperate to pretend.

"Take the throne, and I will follow you," she swore.

One last visit.

Back in the cool shadows of the woods, I closed my eyes and reached for my mother.

Darien?

Yes?

There were many discussions we could have had in that moment. I sighed, *Take care of Nicias for me. I suspect he will come to you soon.*

Hai, what are you doing? Darien demanded.

Fulfilling all your expectations, I answered bitterly. I meant to leave it at that but couldn't stop myself from asking *How could you do this to me, to the world you claim to want to protect? How could you be so blind, to convince Nicias all is well and allow this horror?*

I've told you. My sakkri *are–*

What of my Empress? I asked. *Surely she can see far more than a mongrel can. She must know what will happen if Oliza takes the throne.*

I felt my mother shake her head on the distant Ahnmik as she stared out her window and over the white city. *Cjarsa has more power than you and I combined, but the void frightens her. She fears drowning in its illusions, so she holds back.*

The idea that Cjarsa might have such a powerful weakness was deeply unsettling. *If that's the case, then you're both blind here. Oliza listens to Nicias's counsel, and Nicias would listen to you. You could stop this with a few words to him, if you would* just *trust* me.

I can't. Hai . . . I felt her struggle to choose wording that would be kind. She settled on *You are a falcon despite your father's blood, and I have no way of knowing where your loyalties lie, but I know that they are not with me.*

Sometimes I myself wasn't sure.

Nicias's eyes opened as I returned to his room, my arms laden with a package of freshly baked pastries that Arqueete had given to me on my way back there.

"Good morning," Nicias said.

"Morning." I went to his side, my eyes feasting on the lines of his face—golden lashes, high cheekbones, soft lips, fair skin. "You looked so peaceful I didn't want to wake you."

He smiled, but I knew that he was wary. He had every right to be.

I kissed him, for perhaps the last time.

"I brought breakfast," I said. "We'll need it. I imagine it is going to be a very long day."

CHAPTER 16

Oliza wore plum-violet—the serpiente color of mourning—to her coronation. Officially the color was in honor of her cousin, but Oliza had so much more than that to mourn, and everyone in the audience knew it.

Vere Obsidian was in such a deep shade of blue that it was almost black. I wondered how Oliza felt about her would-be mate's making an effort to avoid the Cobriana royal color, even though the difference in tone was discreet. His white-blond hair had been braided in back but was in no way hidden.

Both Vere and Oliza appeared grave as he helped her onto the dais.

Even once Oliza looked out over the crowd, the marketplace took a long time to hush, as serpiente continued to express their emotions, which ranged from relief at Oliza's return to fury. Even serpents who supported Oliza in general were disturbed by this turn of events.

Nicias, at the foot of the dais, swept the crowd with cool eyes. Only those who knew him well might have recognized how nervous he was.

He was not the only one. Oliza's parents appeared drawn and worn; for twenty years they had dreamed of the day their daughter would take the throne, but this was not the way any parent would have wished that dream to come true.

Sive stood at the far edge of the crowd, shunned by almost everyone but her avian guards; only a lone serpent had elected to stay by her side. Though she held herself straight, her eyes were swollen from crying.

Rosalind was not present. In fact, most of the dancers from the nest were missing. They had attended the coronation of one of their own, but they had chosen to stay by that fallen king's side rather than watch this farce. Their absence pleased me, as it meant my loyalists made up more of the crowd.

How many? I wondered.

There was only one way to find out.

I stepped forward.

Serpents stepped aside, some of them with confusion on their faces, but many with respectful nods, as I moved through the crowd. I kept my face neutral as I approached the bottom of the dais.

"Oliza Shardae Cobriana."

Oliza jumped as I called to her. Nicias, who was nearly next to me now, frowned and said my name. "Hai—"

I boosted myself smoothly onto the dais. "Oliza, a word with you."

"Hai, now is hardly the time," the wyvern replied.

"Now is the *only* time."

"Hai, what do you think you are doing?" Nicias asked.

I spoke clearly so my voice would be heard by the entire crowd.

"My father was the eldest of his generation, older brother to both Zane and Irene Cobriana. I recognized you as Arami, Oliza, because you held that place before my return, but then you gave up that title of your own free will. I recognized Salem because our people respected and followed him, and I wish he could still hold the throne—though from what I can tell of his injuries, he will not recover." The words hung in the air. I knew that every eye and every ear was focused on us at this moment. "I hope, milady wyvern, that you will gracefully step aside, and not attempt to force your way into a position you willingly abandoned."

"This is absurd," Zane said, objecting.

A pair of my followers, both of whom appeared to be soldiers, stepped between the cobra and the stage. "Let her speak," one of them said.

Oliza's voice was frosty when she said, "I stepped down because I knew I could not hold both thrones if I wanted to avoid another war. I never *abandoned* my people when they needed me, and I will not do so now."

"They do not need you now, either." More softly, praying Oliza would hear the truth in my words, I added, "And we both know what you really feared would happen if you took the throne."

Why was I the only one who could see Anhamirak's fire destroying us all? Why was I the only one who could hear the screams as the falcons slaughtered the survivors, leaving only children that the royal house could raise as it wished?

"Hai, this is madness," Oliza said.

Arqueete had come to the front and now pointed out, "It is not mad if it's true. She *is* rightfully Arami."

"*Oliza* is the rightful Arami," someone else shouted.

By now Nicias had climbed onto the stage. He stepped between Oliza and me, the pain of betrayal in his eyes. *"No."* The word was accompanied by angry magic that shuddered through me like the rumble of thunder. "Hai, I will not allow you to—"

I pulled back with a hiss. "Nicias Silvermead, if I am a cobra, then I am not a subject of the royal house of Ahnmik. You have told me this many times. That means *you* are not my prince." I wanted to recall the words the instant I shouted them, wanted to say *It's not true! Please, I meant nothing by it!* Instead, I continued. "Or is this the wish of that house? You say you turned down the falcon throne to stand behind Oliza, Nicias of Ahnmik. Are you here as a guard or a puppeteer?" Nicias was royal falcon born, but I had been Mercy raised. He did not have the experience to turn these allusions around as I spoke quickly, sowing distrust among all the serpiente around us.

"You know that isn't true. I am loyal—"

"Loyal to Oliza?" I asked, with obvious cynicism. "How can you claim to be loyal to the wyvern princess and then ask her to betray the sacred vows she swore to her true mate? How can you say you are loyal to Wyvern's Court and then participate in this sham ceremony in an attempt to—"

"An attempt to protect the throne from—"

"What? Its rightful heir?" I challenged him. "I am not a usurper, Nicias. I am Anjay Cobriana's daughter, and I will not abandon the responsibility of his legacy."

"Nicias, step aside."

Oliza's soft voice sent Nicias away, and I was left looking at the wyvern.

"Oliza, please, do not force this confrontation further," I implored. The crowd around us was beginning to get ugly. My followers were holding back Oliza's family and friends, including Zane Cobriana, but I knew that my loyalists would feel the need to protect me once her father reached the dais. "Neither of us wants blood to be spilled here today."

"I will not allow a *falcon* to usurp the serpiente throne."

I then let myself do something I had never done: I recoiled and shifted into my serpent half form. I had always thought of my cobra fangs and scales as dirty, but when I looked upon Oliza with garnet eyes and hissed, the action felt as natural as a falcon's cry once had.

"Falcon?" I asked. "I have as much cobra blood as you do, *wyvern*. My father would have been Diente had he not been slain by your mother's brother. Is your millennia-old prejudice against *my* mother's blood enough to deny me my rightful place?"

"*You have no rightful place here.*" Oliza was losing her temper and her poise as I twisted around her arguments.

I spun away from her as one of the serpents broke free from the crowd and leapt onto the dais. Sensing the blade and who it was intended for before anyone else noticed it, I pushed Oliza aside.

The blow, which had been meant for the wyvern, struck me in the side, piercing one of my lungs.

"*Stop!*"

My subjects pulled back as I shouted at them. I grabbed the wrist of the serpent who had just tried to end this debate with the death of my opponent, and dragged him forward.

"Oliza is my kin," I said, struggling for breath. "And she is my *heir*. I will not allow you, or any other, to harm her."

Two more serpents scrambled onto the dais. Before I could figure out if they were on my side or Oliza's, Nicias reacted for me. His magic lashed the would-be assassin, the other two serpents on the dais and several others who had been trying to reach us. They all fell back, hissing in pain and anger, and I suppressed a sad smile. In Nicias's attempt to defend his queen, he had cemented her connection to the royal falcon house in the minds of many serpents.

I collapsed to my knees and pulled the knife from my side. Coughing blood, I let my magic fill the wound. Falcons were harder to kill than serpents.

Kneeling, my hands bloody from a wound that had been intended for Oliza, I looked up at the wyvern. I knew the arguments she could make, but either she could not find the words, or she chose not to.

Instead, Oliza took one step back, then another.

"I will not let my pride drag us into a civil war here," she said, struggling to control her anger. "You are the only child of my father's eldest brother, and even though you have never claimed that parentage before, the Cobriana blood still shows true." She looked away as her voice wavered. "I gave my people up once to protect them. I will not let you create the strife I was trying to avoid. As long as my—*our*—people will support you, I will not challenge your claim to the serpiente throne."

She shifted before us all, something Oliza never willingly did. Her wyvern form soared into the skies, every movement betraying her fury and pain.

CHAPTER 17

The crowd beyond the dais watched with a mixture of shock, understanding and—in the case of my followers—arrogance as Oliza left. Some retreated slowly, horrified, but most remained, turning their gazes to me with wide eyes.

Only one serpent still moved forward.

Zane Cobriana stepped, unchallenged, onto the dais. His garnet eyes burned, and I wondered whether he would attempt to speak to me or murder me outright without care for the consequences.

My defense came from an unexpected source. Vere Obsidian, who had stepped back from Oliza when I had ascended the dais, now moved protectively between me and the cobra.

"Get out of the way," Zane snarled.

"Do *not* give me orders, cobra," Vere replied coldly. "I am not your subject. *You* are not king to anyone right now. By your law, you lost that title when Salem took the throne. You have no more authority here than Hai does, and she at least has my respect."

"That is a *falcon*. She has no right to this throne!"

I struggled to my feet. "Yes, I am half falcon. But your daughter is half hawk. If wyvern blood makes an Arami unfit to rule, then you had best search harder for your sister, Irene. Or find yourself a new Naga, for law forbids your having a barren queen when you have no suitable heirs."

"Do not quote serpiente law at me—"

"I believe I need to, since *you* seem to have forgotten it," I said. "You have no right to keep your brother's heir from this throne."

The Cobriana were notorious for their temper, and as I saw the rage in Zane's eyes, I braced myself for a blow.

Vere caught the cobra's wrist.

"If you strike her, I swear to every god in this world, I will destroy you. I think a charge of treason would do quite nicely."

Zane's eyes widened. "She isn't Diente yet."

"Until she declares her mate. Yes, I'm aware of the laws, Zane. I learned them well as we waited for the day when you would name our Adelina *your* Naga. Instead, you broke my aunt's heart and then you executed her. Now you would drag your own Oliza from her beloved mate, and abuse your brother's daughter? And you wonder why the Obsidian guild refuses to kneel to you."

Zane glared. "Who are you to speak as if you understand what went on?"

"I am a subject of Anhamirak," Vere retorted, "and therefore free to speak my mind as I wish. I am a descendent of

Maeve, a child of the Obsidian guild, and therefore well versed in Cobriana politics. I am—"

Are you still courting my father, Vere, or are you courting me now? I remembered asking him. Now I relied on the answer he had given me.

"My mate," I declared. "Or did you think it was only for politics that I would interrupt this ceremony?" I spoke not for Zane but for those in our audience who still might object to this coup. Serpents liked romance; the idea of my challenging Oliza for love would appeal to them.

Vere looked surprised but did not protest. Instead, he wrapped an arm around my waist.

"Diente?"

I glimpsed a hawk out of the corner of my eye, but before I could react, a pale fist caught me under my jaw. Vere barely kept me on my feet as I stumbled backward, shocked, raising one hand to my bleeding lip.

My followers came to my defense, gripping the arms of the woman I now recognized as Danica Shardae, Oliza's mother, the avian queen. Zane had been enough of a threat that no one had even thought to watch for his mate.

"Release her!" I shouted to my guards, but they just looked at each other skeptically. "She is Oliza's mother. She has every right to be upset, and even if she did not, I have not done all this only to begin the war again by harming the Tuuli Thea!" At my glare, they reluctantly let go of the infuriated hawk, but this time they kept their attention on her.

Zane went to his mate's side as she spoke to me.

"Throughout my childhood, I was taught that a serpent couldn't be trusted," she said through clenched teeth. "Thousands of years of war were justified by that premise. Now my king, my pair bond, is a cobra. I love him. I trust him. I have learned that there is no evil inherent in serpiente blood.

"The head of my guard, Kel Silvermead," she continued, "is a falcon. She and her alistair, and their son, Nicias, are among the most loyal subjects Wyvern's Court could ever hope to have. So I know there is no innate flaw in falcons, either.

"But you, Diente, you are nothing but a soulless, bloodless *mongrel*. What you have done today . . ."

"It is better to be a soulless, bloodless mongrel," I replied cuttingly, "than an emotionless hawk who can't step down off her superior throne to look at the truth. Oliza is your daughter, and I know you want to protect her, but this is not her place."

"Oliza is more than my daughter," the Tuuli Thea said. "She is more than a princess; she is a symbol of a dream that took thousands of years to bring about, which you, raised on your island, can barely comprehend. When my daughter abdicated, she gave her crown to Sive and Salem, and her trust in them was enough to keep this land together. But now . . . now that's over. My people will leave Wyvern's Court. No matter what Sive or I may say, your betrayal will split this world in two."

"Better they leave in peace than stay and burn." At least this way they would have their precious freedom. It would take time for the serpiente to find their equilibrium again, and in the meantime there would be fights both within the serpiente and between them and the avians, but I had to believe that eventually the balance would return. Fate willing, they would never learn how close they had danced to a future in which the freedoms they worshipped were ripped away and replaced by lies, manipulations and rewritten history from the falcon empire.

Nicias stepped past me without a glance and touched Zane's shoulder respectfully. "Sir, milady Shardae, I am worried I will not be able to keep the crowd back if the three of you stay here. I do not believe that most in the crowd would harm you, but we have already had one would-be assassin."

Zane looked around with a heartbroken expression. Danica did not turn her golden-fire eyes from mine. They both knew what Nicias was really saying: This battle was over. The serpiente people had not rejected me, and that meant that no matter how much they hated this turn of events, they had no right to eject me from this dais.

"I am your kin, and I love this world," I said. I sincerely meant every word. "I will not betray it. I swear that to you both."

"Dien—sir?" Nicias said again, at the last moment changing his address from the title this cobra no longer held. "Lady Shardae?"

Slowly, the royal pair withdrew from the dais, leaving me alone with Vere Obsidian and a hundred pairs of serpiente eyes on us.

Too softly for those beyond the dais to hear, Vere whispered drily, "I never realized that you and I were so close."

"I have seen what will happen if Oliza rules," I explained. I planned my next words carefully before I spoke. "You asked me once what horrors I saw. Salem's death was only the beginning. I care for this world, and I am determined that it will not experience the bloodbath I can see so easily in its path. I have no desire to rule, but if I must—and I do believe that I must—then I want you beside me. It is the least I can do for you. And if you truly wish to honor my father, and help his daughter, then it is the most you can do for me."

Vere's expression was one of sweet concern, but his words were cool. "Aside from your lovely attempt at emotional blackmail, why would I wish to be your king, falcon?"

"Because you wanted to be king before," I answered. "You accepted Oliza's suit. I can match the terms she offered you."

I needed to block the path to every future in which the child Keyi could exist.

Among the serpiente, lovers came and went, but a couple sworn as mates never strayed. Those vows were even more sacred among the Nesera'rsh and so the Obsidian guild. If I could bind this man to me, I knew he would not visit Oliza's bed while I still lived.

"I feel like I am bartering for bread, not hearing a proposal."

"I can only offer what I have," I told him softly. "I cannot swear undying love. You would know it was a lie. I know that this land has never done you favors, and you certainly owe the Cobriana nothing, but I need you. Wyvern's Court needs you."

He nodded slowly. "Very well . . . cobra. Let's dance this step. Just lead the way."

I turned, at long last, to the enraptured crowd. I found myself shaking and had to lean against Vere for support.

My people were confused, frightened, utterly overwhelmed. Some of them had actively supported me, but most of them simply did not know what to do.

I did not know how to comfort them, so I chose honesty. "I love this world. I will not abandon her now that she needs me. If Salem wakes, I will willingly acknowledge him as my Diente. The rumors that led to his fall were false, as the avian queen-to-be herself has attested, and he is still the rightful king of this land. If Irene returns with another child, I will acknowledge that child as my heir. I will not allow the Cobriana line to diminish."

I said this to address the question of what would happen to their royal line when it was mixed with the blood of falcons and white vipers.

I said it also because Ahnmik's magic was too strong in me. I did not know if I would ever be able to have a child, and I certainly did not wish to rule until the end of time, as the falcon royals seemed content to do.

"I stand before you and swear a solemn vow to do what I must to protect this land, *my* land, until that day. I have also sworn to honor the promises made by Oliza regarding the Obsidian guild, which has been outcast from our society for too long. Wyvern's Court is meant to be a place without old hatred.

"And so I wish to present to you my mate, your Nag . . ." I hesitated, not sure how to introduce the white viper. Members of the Obsidian guild guarded their names, never sharing them with anyone but those to whom they were deeply connected.

"Vere Obsidian," he provided, loudly enough for the crowd to hear. More softly, he said to me, "Make it worth it, Diente."

It's done.

And yet there was so much more to come.

CHAPTER 18

"I need to speak to my people and explain to them what happened here," Vere said to me as we stepped down off the dais. Two of my loyalists moved to flank us, guarding us from any of Oliza's or Zane's supporters who might have taken offense to any—or all—of what had just occurred.

"I'm still not entirely sure what *did* happen," Vere admitted. "I'm trusting you that there was a reason for this."

I nodded. "I assure you, there was. I will try to explain when we have a few moments alone."

For now, it would have to wait. Arqueete and Salokin found their way to the front of the crowd and knelt before me.

Arqueete grasped my hand. "Diente, I . . ." The rest of her words were lost to me as I instead heard what she had said to Salokin two days before.

*   *   *

"No one will believe it," Salokin said.

"No one needs to believe it except Prentice," Arqueete responded practically. *"Do you really think that raven will stop to think about . . ."*

The vision faded, but I had heard enough. I withdrew my hand, taking a step back.

"Arqueete, Salokin . . ." Both serpents looked nervous when they heard my tone. "You're both under arrest, for conspiracy to commit regicide. In short, for treason."

"I . . ." Salokin's blue eyes widened. "Milady—"

"But we did it for you!" Arqueete protested. "And look where you are! It isn't treason to support the rightful heir to the throne."

"You *murdered* Salem Cobriana."

"We never touched him!" Salokin cried. "You were there. Prentice attacked him."

"I was also there in the market when you spread the rumors that sent Prentice after him. You might not have held the blade in your own hand, but you planned its use."

"No." Arqueete shook her head. "Milady, please, I beg your mercy. I did it only for you."

"My *Mercy?*" I echoed. "Be grateful I have none. Serpiente law says you will have a trial for this crime, and witnesses to speak on your behalf, if you can find any. It is more than I want to give you." I summoned one of my self-appointed guards, who was looking at Salokin and Arqueete in horror. "Arrest them. Bring them to the nest; Salem was not only a cobra but a dancer, and turning these two over to nest justice is the least I can do."

Salokin begged, "Please, Hai, don't do this."

I shook my head. "If you wish to redeem your honor, be honest with the dancers," I suggested. "If you wish to die a coward as well as a traitor, beg me further."

He went white and bowed his head before allowing my soldier to escort him to the nest.

"Milady, someone else to speak to you," another of my followers said to me.

I turned as if underwater. I did not need to be warned of Nicias's approach; I could sense it. Vere, who had stood silently beside me as I had dealt with the traitors, now stepped back to give us some space.

"Please, don't," I said softly.

"How convenient," Nicias observed, "to be able to execute the weapons you used to win this throne."

"You know I would never have harmed Salem," I said. "You may never forgive me for not allowing Oliza to return, but someday, you will at least believe that I did not wish for this."

He shook his head dismissively.

Oh, gods. My sweet Ecl, Ahnmik, I wish I could reach for you now to take me back into my numbness.

I lifted my gaze to his blue one and fought to keep the tears from spilling. *My Nicias, my light, you took me from the darkness.* I whispered silently to Nicias, and felt him listening briefly before he started to block me out again. *You took me from my black tower and taught me to feel again. Don't look at me with that fury, that awful look of betrayal.*

"I had no choice," I said aloud.

"No choice; of course."

"Nicias, *please*, you know as well as I do why Oliza cannot rule."

He shook his head again. "I don't know anything anymore. *Anything.* Hai, *I brought you here.* I defended you. I fell asleep with you in my arms and I thought—" He cleared his throat. "You slipped away while I slept to usurp my queen's throne, and now you dare tell me that you *had no choice*?"

The anguish in his voice was even worse than the anger. "I have to go," I whispered.

Fury smoldered in his gaze, and his body was rigid with the effort it took to keep his voice level as he continued. "Before you leave: I did not come here to criticize you. That isn't my *place.* I just came here to request that you release me from my obligations to Wyvern's Court."

"Nicias—"

He ignored my plea. "I do not feel it is appropriate for me to serve under the next Diente when I swore my loyalty to Oliza. I have been offered a position among the Royal Flight, effective once I leave."

No, I wanted to say, *I give no such permission.*

He would leave anyway, though. This was just a formality. Nothing I said would keep him here, after what I had done to him.

Forgive me, my love, I called silently. The words fell upon deaf ears.

Nicias did nothing more than frown, but the falcon shuddered at the prince of Ahnmik's obvious displeasure and turned to address Nicias's mate with a trembling voice.

"My Lady." His downcast eyes were unable to conceal his terror. "Please, forgive a foolish man his ill-conceived words."

"Do you apologize for my benefit," she asked, "or for my prince's?"

Ahnmik's magic would not let this falcon lie, no matter how much she wished it would. The man looked at his aona'ra *and cringed. Araceli's heir was not in a forgiving mood.*

Nicias would join the Royal Flight for a short time, but it would not be long before he would become restless. He would go to Ahnmik for valiant reasons, but the city would turn him into what he most hated—and it would be my fault.

How long would it take him, I wondered, to change into the cold, jaded prince I kept seeing lately? How long would it take him to forget Oliza—and me—and pick this other woman as his lover?

I could have saved him from that fate. I could have given him back Oliza. But the price, the destruction of Wyvern's Court, was one I knew he would never have chosen to pay.

So I damned him.

"Permission granted."

Nicias nodded. "Thank you." For a moment I thought he sounded regretful, but I did not know whether it was for leaving me or for saving me in the first place.

It's done, fateful words, echoed in the beat of his wings as he fled and in my pounding heartbeat.

"I'm sorry," Vere whispered. "But if what you have done is indeed for the best, he *will* someday realize that. First, though, he needs to calm down."

I shook my head. "I fear that by the time he calms down, he may be a very different man."

Vere started to reach for me, then hesitated, his mind surely on the peregrine who occupied my heart. I took the white viper's hand in mine, needing some kind of comfort but feeling just as awkward about it.

We had been . . . Had we been friends? I didn't even know if I could use that term. Now suddenly we had agreed to be mates. Even our reasons differed.

I turned to lean against Vere, closing my eyes for a moment. I did not love him, but as Oliza had said, he was a kind man. Of the two of us, I was far more likely to be cruel.

I opened my eyes again, prepared to suggest we move out of the marketplace, when suddenly I saw the child Keyi only a few feet away from us. Her pale blue eyes were gazing up at Vere with fascination. Her golden hair was rumpled, as if she had been playing.

I felt myself go cold.

"What is it?" Vere whispered as I pulled away from him.

Then he seemed to turn, and lift the girl in his arms, spinning her about.

Why?

I had done everything I could do, *everything*. What assassin's knife was going to find me, to allow this girl to live? I could think of no other way I would let her *a'she* come to pass.

She was laughing, this girl with so much blood on her hands.

I looked at the serpents who had surrounded me only moments before, and saw them all still and silent, their bodies glistening with the golden magic that would burn through this land like a storm.

I threw my mind into the power, screaming, *Why?*

Ecl, my love.

Ahnmik, my master.

Anhamirak, my bane, please, I must know! There must be a way to stop this fire.

Vere caught my hands, trying to call me back to the real

world. I felt his magic from Ahnmik soothe mine, even as Anhamirak's power shivered across my skin like . . .

Fire.

Like Oliza's wyvern.

Then the vision of the girl turned to me, and her eyes lit up as she said, "Mommy!"

Oliza was not the only one whose magic was unbalanced, made dangerous by Anhamirak's flames.

No.

Fate could not be so cruel.

When had it ever been gentle?

I shoved back from Vere, hard enough that only a serpent's reflexes kept him from falling. I felt the murmur in the crowd more than I heard it.

When I turned to run, people tried to stop me. Maya grabbed my arm, demanding an explanation, before Opal dragged her away.

I pushed past my followers and my enemies in a panicked daze, fleeing toward the only place I could think of: Wyvern's Nest.

CHAPTER 19

Only a few feet from the nest, I slammed into Velyo as the wolf stepped in front of me.

"Diente," he said, greeting me with a nod.

"Frektane," I replied, gritting my teeth. I tried to step around him, and he blocked me. "What do you want?"

"I wanted to offer my congratulations," he said, "and I suppose an apology. I misjudged you."

"Fine. Forgiven," I said. "Now move aside."

"You look upset," he observed.

"And in a hurry," I returned.

"You did the right thing."

The right thing—this from Velyo Frektane, of all people. "I want no comfort from a man who murdered his own father to ascend to the throne."

"I did it for the good of my pack—just as you have done this for the good of Wyvern's Court. Oliza's weakness would have made her—"

"If Wyvern's Court had been ready for a wyvern queen, Oliza Shardae Cobriana—and her Naga, Betia Frektane—would have been the greatest monarchs this land had ever known," I snapped. "They are both strong, just and capable leaders . . . and they will prove it," I continued as the vision came to me, "when Betia succeeds *you* as alpha of the Frektane."

Velyo scoffed. "Your prophecies have become muddled again, Hai. There is no way I would allow that deviant back into our pack."

I had seen in *sakkri* this wolf with his angry hands on Oliza's mate. I had seen him try to repeat the crime with the wyvern. I had stolen Oliza's throne from her only minutes earlier, but there was one gift I could give to her and Betia now, so I gave it. "You want a prophecy, Velyo?" *Sometimes, speaking of a vision can set into motion the very events one is trying to prevent.* Or in this case, trying to cause. "Betia and Oliza *will* become the much-beloved queens of the Frektane tribe. Their son, an orphaned wolf cub they will adopt within the next few years, will inherit the title later. And you will have a say in none of it—because you will be dead within the next six months, at the jaws of one of the wolves you call your allies."

As I spoke the words, I felt Fate shiver, the future realigning itself until the possible events I had seen became a near certainty. Paranoia would eat at Velyo, and he would turn his fear on his allies until they would be forced to exterminate him.

"Enjoy your future," I said. "Now, I have my own to attend to." I pushed forward, shoving the horrified wolf out of the way, and stumbled through the doorway of the dancer's nest.

Inside, I was struck by the silence. Usually this place was

full of graceful bodies and joyous sounds, but now all I heard was a single voice.

Rosalind, Salem's mate, was singing a haunting, wordless melody. The others were silently dancing, their movements slow and careful.

They were praying, offering their worship to the gods in exchange for the health of one of their own.

The instant Rosalind noticed me, the mood shifted from sorrowful to angry.

"You aren't welcome here, falcon," she said. Her eyes were glazed with tears, and I could feel her pain like hail against my skin. "I don't care if you *are* Diente. You have no right to be here."

"I need to see Salem."

"So you can finish what your supporters started?" Rosalind said accusingly.

"So I can try to save him!" Serpents jumped, as startled as I was by how desperate I sounded. The dancers were the only rulers of their nest. My own magic would stop me if I tried to force my way past them.

Before Rosalind could respond, A'isha, the nest leader, placed a hand on her shoulder. "What can you do for him?"

"I don't know," I admitted. "But I have to—"

"We can't trust her!" Rosalind protested. "For all we know, it is her magic that is keeping him in this state."

A'isha shook her head. "I can't know your intentions for certain," she said to me, "but I will let you pass. If Salem's guard disagrees, you will leave."

"Thank you."

I pushed past, shaking off Rosalind when she tried to stop me. Behind me, I heard A'isha trying to calm the fearful woman.

I descended the stairs to the private rooms beneath the nest and found Salem's room easily. When I opened the door, Nicias looked up at me with disdain.

"Oh, gods," I whispered. "Nicias . . ."

"Get out of here," he ordered.

He knew that my vows to him were what kept me in this world, knew that my magic would tear at me to obey him. I fell to my knees to keep from turning around.

"You have to listen to me," I begged, fear, need and pain all too clear in my voice. "Oliza *cannot* take the throne. For her to do so would be disaster. You haven't seen— Dear Ahnmik, help me speak true and clearly," I prayed. "You haven't seen the visions I've been haunted by. You haven't seen Oliza murdered by her own child. You haven't seen Wyvern's Court burned to ash by Anhamirak's fire, or by the falcons when they come. . . ." My voice trembled. "I heard you scream, too, Nicias, my— Please, believe me, I would do everything in my power to keep you from that pain. I know you fear that *sakkri* can mislead, but not these," I whispered. "I have never seen visions this strong, this sure. I've tried and tried and I can't keep this land from burning."

He crossed the room as if he couldn't help himself, and lifted me to my feet. Even if he hated me, Nicias wasn't the type of man who could stand by and let a woman grovel.

His hands did not linger on mine. Coldly, he said, "So you set yourself up as queen of a land you never wanted. Then why are you here?"

"Because I can't rule, either," I whispered. I looked at Salem. "I swear to you, Nicias, I have never betrayed you. I swear it by blood, by fire, by flesh, by steel, by Ecl and by Ahnmik and by all that is and never will be. . . . I swear I have never lied to you and I have never betrayed you. I breathe this scorched air *for you*. Now, please, *believe me*. In every vision I see, this land falls. In every future I look to, I see you screaming. Salem Cobriana must take the throne, or our world *burns*."

"Ours?"

"You made your world mine," I said. "When you pulled me from Ecl, you gave me this land. At first I hated you for that. Now . . . I don't want this land to become the falcon crystal I see whenever I turn around. Let me try to help Salem."

"You couldn't help him before," he argued. "How can you help him now?"

"I'll dive deeper. . . . I don't know, maybe I can't do anything, but I need to try again. It's all I can do."

He stepped to the side, letting me past. When I moved toward the silent cobra, Nicias touched my arm.

"I'll try to hold you, to keep you from going too far."

I shook my head. "Don't pull me back. His life means more than mine."

Presuming there was any life left to save.

CHAPTER 20

Oh, gods, help me. Diving into Salem's body again *hurt.* He wanted to die, but the magic I had wrapped into him previously kept him on this side of existence. His heart wanted to stop, but my power kept it beating.

His spirit was curled somewhere in the darkness, screaming in pain as it struggled to flee its corpse. Fear and agony ripped through me as his flesh prayed for release.

Had Salem been anyone else, I would have given him a gentle death, faced with such pleas. I was tempted to do so even now, but there was too much at stake.

This world needs you, I cried, begging him to return.

But how could he return when his body wouldn't take him? It wasn't . . . right. Stripped of its magic, it had no life, no place for a heart and a mind and a soul. It yearned for Brysh's embrace, after which there would be only silence and peace.

For him. For us, there would be only pain.

Come to me, I commanded, straining with every ounce of

my own magic. *Come to me.* I tried to wrap the words around him but felt him slipping away.

I cursed the *am'haj* poison. I slid my power over the ruined edges of his magic, trying to make him whole again, but Ahnmik can only destroy, and I had never had control over the hint of Anhamirak in my blood.

I tried to soothe Salem's pain and coax his terrified spirit back into this body, promising anything if he would return to this land. I felt him starting to fall into his final rest instead of rising.

I drew back and felt him shriek.

Salem could not survive without magic.

Wyvern's Court could not survive without Salem.

And Wyvern's Court needed to survive.

Therefore, Salem's body needed magic.

Suddenly I felt calm.

I had tried being gentle, coaxing and soothing and begging in much the same way that Ecl had whispered to me for years. *Come to me, and I will let you rest,* the void called. *Come to me, and I will take care of you. I will comfort you, and you will be at peace.*

But Anhamirak's power wasn't rooted in peace, gentleness and quiet entreaties. A cobra's magic, my father's magic, was what burned in me every moment of my life. It was fire and chaos; it was freedom, savage and natural, beyond civilization and law.

And it was desperation.

I slammed power into the cobra now, drowning his body in all the energy I had at my disposal. I held back nothing, baring every part of myself as I forced his flesh and soul to do as I willed.

Desperation was all I had left.

Finally I felt something in him react to the assault, drawn by the flicker of my father's magic. I had never been able to control Anhamirak's power, but now I used it as a lure, enticing Salem not with promises of rest—serpents didn't *rest*—but with heat.

Now I have you. I twined myself around and through every particle of his being, using Anhamirak to hold him close and Ahnmik to slice through the bonds between flesh and magic. I severed the rotten, tattered remnants of magic left by the *am'haj* poison, and felt Salem instinctively clutch at the familiar, healthy magic in my blood.

One more cut and—

I screamed as I felt the fabric of my reality rip. I struggled not to flee from the ice storm that struck me as my power slid away from me, seeking a more comfortable home.

Cold . . . so cold. Once, I had called Ecl cold, but that had been a blessed numbness compared to this. . . .

Back on the ice, I felt it cut into my hands and my knees as it began to shatter, as I fell into the darkness, choking on the frozen black water.

Down, someone said to me, a voice that sounded so familiar, so comforting. *Dive. Now.*

The beasts that used to dwell beneath the ice, forever drawn toward Anhamirak's warmth, ignored me. As I sank into the void, images of the past fluttered before me.

I walked through the white city as a child and spoke to spirits others couldn't see. Oh, how the world shone so brilliantly. The voices of the Mercy who raised me faded as I listened to the songs the city wove. I could hear the colors of the sea and taste the moonlight and feel the shifting strands of Fate all around me.

*   *   *

"When might I be able to see the Empress?"

This cobra had no fear at all. Though Anjay had been carried across the ocean by Pure Diamond falcons, who could as easily have dropped him into the sea, he had held his head high from the instant he had set foot on the white island–a place no Kiesha'ra had ever stood before.

"When she decides you are worth speaking to," Darien replied.

"How am I to convince her of my worth if you never let me so much as walk in the city?"

My lady?

Let him see our land, Cjarsa whispered through Darien's mind. Give him beauty. There will be none in the world to which he must return.

"I have always loved you, Darien." Years later, and still Cjarsa and my mother argued. "Always favored you. Always bent Ahnmik's rigid laws for you, though Ecl shrieks at me every time those laws are broken. I could not let a mongrel be trained in this land. Hai would never have survived if I had tried. But have you no faith at all that I might have worked toward this hena'she?"

My mother turned her back on her Empress, though she could not close her ears to Cjarsa's words or close her heart to her own hope.

"If I had let you care for your daughter, if I had not sent Kel to bring you to me and thus forced her into exile, if I had not twisted Fate as I willed with each step of the way, this Nicias would never have been born. Your daughter would never have risen from the darkness–"

"No." I interrupted them now.

Cjarsa was not surprised that I had been present and listening.

"It is little enough," she pointed out, "compared to your machinations to save Wyvern's Court. Why does it seem so impossible that I might work to save one child—the only child of my favored companion?"

"If you dared walk the line between Mehay and Ecl, where Fate is woven . . . but you do not. You fear it. You have feared it since the day you saw the first of your followers slide into Ecl. Araceli's terror led her to create the avian people. Yours led you to write the laws of this land, to bind you to it so Ecl could not take you."

"Enough!"

I had spoken without thinking, as if in a trance, but Cjarsa's command snapped me back from it.

"As you wish, my lady," I whispered.

Ecl'gah. Illusion, all of it.

"I am sorry to distress you," I said. I remembered the terror that had gripped me the day Nicias had first invaded my private illusion. His soul had stained that still and silent realm forever.

Cjarsa had no other world, no other place, and no one to call her from this white realm.

I did.

"Hai? Where are you, Hai?"

*   *   *

I could go back to Nicias. I paused, wondering. Memories of the past and the present poured through me, but I knew I could go back to him.

"Hai, listen to my voice."

So I did. It was simple. The water was cold, and deep, and dark, but I found its center, and there . . . I was.

CHAPTER 21

I opened my eyes, though it did me little good. I thought I was still in the private room beneath the dancer's nest, but the lamps had burned out long before, leaving no light to see by. What I did know was that I was once again in Nicias's arms. I felt him stir, waking at the same time that I did.

"What happens if there comes a day when I'm not here to save you?" he asked me.

"Then . . . I'll find my way back on my own."

I struggled to gather my thoughts, remembering the last scene with Cjarsa. Had I really argued with the white Lady of Ahnmik? Or had that been another vision of another future? What possible future could I have in which I would so brazenly challenge my Empress?

My head began to pound as I remembered what we had been doing here.

"Salem . . ."

I pulled away from Nicias and closed my eyes for a

moment, trying to focus past the pain at my temples. The cobra wasn't here. I would have been able to sense him even with my unfocused magic.

"He's gone," Nicias said, coming to the same conclusion.

My limbs ached as I pushed myself to my feet, swaying before Nicias stood beside me and steadied me.

Together we groped our way through the darkness, toward the doorway and up the stairs, until we blinked at the sudden light and noise of the dancer's nest.

Before my eyes had a chance to adjust to the brightness from the central fire, Rosalind intercepted us, her posture guarded as she looked from me to Nicias.

"Salem's awake," I said. I could tell just by looking at the dancer before me. She was wearing a simple outfit made of two carefully wrapped and tied *melos*, one deep emerald in color, and one black with green stitching. At her temple was a symbol meaning *victory*. It was not an outfit for mourning.

"He is," she replied.

Other dancers had drifted toward us, though they left Rosalind plenty of space.

"Is he . . . well?" I remembered a jumble of sensations and panicked thoughts. I had no idea what I had done, in my desperation, to make the cobra wake, or what the consequences might be.

She hesitated, frowning.

Nicias understood before I did. "Hai isn't your enemy," he told Rosalind. "Salem was dying. If he is up now, it is entirely through Hai's efforts. She risked more than you can possibly imagine to go after him."

Rosalind cringed, looking away and then immediately back at me. "I'm sorry. With all that has happened . . . I don't understand any of it. From the moment that Oliza announced that she was going to abdicate—" She shook her head, making her long auburn hair ripple. "No. It started long before then."

It had started the day the young serpiente Arami, Zane Cobriana, and the avian heir to the Tuuli Thea, Danica Shardae, first sat together, in a room in the Mistari homelands, and decided that they would find a way to bring peace—no matter the cost.

Rosalind struggled to compose herself. "You were both unconscious for several days. We didn't know if you had fought, if you were responsible for Salem's recovery, or if you were our enemies. No one knew what to do. We spoke to your mother, Nicias, and she said there was probably nothing we *could* do, so we left you undisturbed. I am very glad that you are awake now."

"As am I," I said. "Where can we find Salem?"

"I'll bring you to him," Rosalind offered.

We found Salem in the market, making the rounds of the merchants there.

"We have been struggling to show solidarity with the avians," Rosalind explained as we approached the restored Diente. "Zane and Danica have been around to help, as well, but it has really been Sive who has done the most." I wondered if Rosalind had any doubts about Salem's relationship with the hawk, but I pushed the thoughts away as she embraced her mate. "Hai and Nicias are awake," she said unnecessarily.

Salem took a moment to assess the situation before saying, "I've heard many different theories on what happened. Do I have you to thank for my recovery, Hai?"

"Wyvern's Court needed its Diente."

His voice hardened somewhat. "I understand you briefly assumed that position in my absence."

"I had no intention of harming Oliza, nor did I desire to usurp any throne," I said frankly. "Wyvern's Court is my home. I did what I could to try to protect it."

Slowly, the cobra nodded. "Oliza tried to help calm people after you fell ill, but she was even less trusted than I was. She wasn't welcome in Wyvern's Court."

I winced. "I'm sorry I caused that hardship. I will make certain to clarify what happened, quickly."

Our conversation had drawn the attention of everyone in the market. Many of the people who watched us were my allies.

As odd as it felt to consider this cobra kin, it felt almost right when I let out a long breath and went down on one knee before Salem.

"Hai, this isn't necessary," he protested.

"Yes, it is," I said. "I was not behind the attempt to assassinate you, but I was the motive for it. If you were *shm' Ahnmik*, you would have me killed."

"I'm no falcon," he whispered.

"I have allies in your kingdom, Diente."

"So do I—but I wouldn't if I went about executing everyone who could possibly be a threat. You're innocent, Hai. You're *more* than innocent; you saved my life. Please, cousin, stand up."

It was the first time he had ever acknowledged any relationship between us. I didn't know how to reply.

He took my hands as I stood.

"Wyvern's Court has gone through a lot. Your help—and the help of your allies—would be greatly appreciated," Salem admitted. "When I stepped out of the dancer's nest without you beside me, even people who had protested your taking the crown were horrified. There was no way to convince them that we had not harmed you. Hopefully you will be able to calm them, now that you are awake."

"Have Salokin and Arqueete come to trial?" I asked.

"They both confessed," he said. "Out of loyalty to you, they said."

"And Prentice?"

"I asked that he be returned to the avians for trial. He was convicted of treason, grounded and exiled." Salem shook his head and moved on. "Those trials were the easiest part of the last few days. Most of our hours have been devoted to keeping people from rioting. If a few of your followers—the candlemaker, and a handful of others—had not stepped forward to speak to your loyalists, I do not think we would have been able to keep control at all."

"Gren?" Nicias asked. He had been so quiet behind me all this time that his voice startled me.

Salem nodded. "Maya was actually the one who spoke to me first. She had a few questions."

"You know who she is, then?" I asked.

"We spoke at length," he answered discreetly. "I don't know that I can do anything for her—I don't dare risk inciting Ahnmik's wrath—but at some point I would appreciate your council on the subject. Maya, Gren, Opal and Spark worked to keep Wyvern's Court from falling apart while you were gone. I don't want to ignore them now."

I admitted, "If I had not spoken to them, it is quite

possible that all four of them would have participated in the plot to have you killed. On Ahnmik, they would all be guilty of treason."

"And in Wyvern's Court, they are responsible only for the crimes they have committed, and for their actions, I owe them thanks." His tone clearly said he considered the discussion over and further debate irrelevant. "Though I am glad you convinced them to be on my side, and not the other."

I shrugged, still not used to his gratitude.

From above came a shriek—a sound that both chilled me and made my heart race. Salem, Nicias and I lifted our eyes to take in a quartet of falcons: three gyrfalcons and a peregrine.

The group banked, circling once before it dove, and then the Empress Cjarsa's Mercy landed before us.

CHAPTER 22

Nicias started to draw his blade but hesitated as he beheld the gyrfalcon in the front. My mother. In Wyvern's Court. I started to step forward, but Nicias stopped me with a hand on my shoulder. His eyes focused upon the peregrine beside Darien, and I heard the ring of steel as he drew his weapon defensively upon seeing Lillian, the woman who only a few months before had been his lover.

The falcons fell back into formal postures, with their feet planted slightly apart and their right hands grasping their left wrists behind their backs, under the wings of their Demi forms. They did not acknowledge Nicias or me, focusing first on Salem.

"Salem Cobriana," Darien said, "I understand you are Diente now?"

Two of Salem's guards had materialized from the surrounding market, drawn by the falcons' cries, and stood beside him now as he said, "I am. And you are?"

The gyrfalcon answered, *"Shm'Ahnmik'la'Darien'jaes'-oisna'ona'saniet'mana'Leonecl'mana'heah.* And this is my working partner, *Lillian'jaes'mael'ona'saniet'mana'heah."* Darien and Lillian, working together?

Why were the Empress's elite messengers here? They had not come when Oliza had abdicated or when Salem had nearly been killed. Why *now?* I did not know whether to be overjoyed or frightened. The presence of the Empress's Mercy in this land could not be good.

Salem glanced at Nicias.

"What is the white Lady's Mercy doing in Wyvern's Court?" Nicias asked.

Only now did the two women turn to him. "You speak for the Diente?"

"I speak for my king," Nicias replied boldly.

Darien laughed a little, finally breaking from formality. "You, Nicias, are the only falcon on this earth who would dare call a cobra your king while standing before the finest of the Empress's Mercy."

"And you, Darien," Nicias said, "are the only falcon on this earth who would be forgiven for treason as many times as you have been."

She gave a little bow. "I am as loyal to my Empress as I should be. Now, to answer your question . . ." Her eyes, as they lifted to mine, were liquid silver. "The Empress felt a falcon wake."

Nicias argued, "Hai has been awake for months. Why come now?" This time, Lillian laughed, a sound that made Nicias tense. Her voice was soft and musical but cold as she spoke to the man who could have been her prince in another world. "You misunderstand," she said. "It did not matter to the Empress when a mongrel dancer opened her eyes. She was perhaps glad of it, because she favored the cobra child, but that was all, and it did not trouble her when again your Hai fell and reawakened several days ago, save that she felt the harm done to royal blood when you, Nicias, tried to save her.

"What interests *ona'la'Cjarsa*," Lillian continued, "is the shift in the magic she felt a day ago. A shift that felt like the birth of a pure-blood falcon."

"Then it isn't me you felt," I said bitterly, starting to turn away. My mother still had not even acknowledged her relationship to me, and I had no desire to speak with the woman who had once been Nicias's lover.

"Isn't it?" Darien whispered. "Hai . . . *shm'Ahnmik'-la'Hai-ra'o'la*." She called me a falcon and her daughter, and those words made me hesitate. "You spin *sakkri* stronger than most of the Mercy, mindwalk as simply as breathing, and have survived Ecl. Your features betray your cobra blood—the black hair and garnet eyes are not of Ahnmik—but it is Ahnmik's magic that holds you."

"It is Ahnmik's magic that has always cursed me," I returned.

My mother shook her head. She looked at Salem and asked him, "Do you know what my daughter has done for you, cobra?" When Salem did not respond, she asked Nicias, "Do you, Nicias?"

Nicias turned toward me, but I knew he could not tell what it was he saw.

Darien stepped forward and took my hand. "Your magic will never be as powerful as it was when it danced to Anhamirak's flame . . . when it was sparked by that which you gave to your king." She looked back at Salem and, almost angrily, informed him, "Would you tear open your soul and give it to another, cobra? That is what my daughter has done for you—given to you that which her father gave to her. Anhamirak's magic—the magic our poison destroyed in your blood."

Salem's eyes widened. Instinctively, hearing my mother's words, I tried to call upon my own serpent form—

And found nothing.

I tried to draw across my skin the black scales—

And found nothing.

Desperately, I sought any magic I had left with which to change from this form—

And screamed as my body tried to return to the broken, battered falcon I had lost when I had fallen from the sky above the white city years before.

Nicias caught me, sheathing his blade to hold me in his arms, his magic reaching out to soothe me.

One last try. I reached this time for the magic that came from Ahnmik. I felt it ripple through me, rubbing against Nicias's power like a cat seeking attention. He jumped, startled, and I pulled back.

He glanced at Lillian, then back at me. "Darien is right. You feel like a pure-blood falcon now."

Lillian smiled a little. "At least I made a lasting impression."

"Like a knife blade," Nicias snapped. Then he dropped his gaze, shaking his head. "You were acting under orders."

"Mostly," Lillian replied. "If it makes you feel better, my interest in you wasn't all feigned."

"That doesn't really help, and it doesn't make me trust you now. Either of you," he added, turning to Darien, "no matter how you might have helped me in the past. You felt a pure-blood falcon wake. Cjarsa felt her wake. Now what do you want with her?"

With very few exceptions, a falcon was not allowed to live off the island. Nicias had been granted his pardon because he was Araceli's blood. His parents had sacrificed their magic and their falcon forms to stay here. What would Cjarsa ask of me?

Will she let me stay?

Did I *want* her to let me stay?

To see the white city again, to walk through it, not as *quemak* but with magic as pure as all the rest . . .

But I still did not have my Demi or falcon form, and even if my magic was untainted now, the rest of my body was not. I was too dark; my father's cobra blood was still too evident.

Still . . .

"Naturally," Lillian replied, "the Empress wants her own returned."

"No," I whispered. I had never thought I would say that word in this context, but it slipped off my lips. "Wyvern's Court is my home now. I have—"

I broke off, about to say I *have responsibilities here.*

I had worked so hard for the court that leaving would feel like abandoning it. If I disappeared now, without a word to the serpiente, my followers would forever distrust Salem. I needed to stay, at least a little longer.

And then a little longer. I knew how this went. I knew the Cobriana; one did not easily name oneself one of them only to walk away. Even Oliza's abdication had been for her people. If I didn't walk away now, I would never be able to.

"You have . . . ?" my mother asked when I did not finish.

"Never mind."

"Our orders are to bring you to the city," one of the other falcons said. "Why are we even having this discussion?"

Lillian and my mother looked at each other, a meaningful glance that made Lillian sigh and say, "Please come with us willingly."

"May I have time to consider?" I asked, though I did not know why. I had no choices to consider except whether to fight or obey.

"Yes," my mother said, at the same moment that one of the others said, "No."

"Darien," Lillian warned.

"Yes, Lillian?" My mother's voice was falsely sweet.

"Hai," Lillian said, "please come home with us. Your place is on Ahnmik. You have power here, I know, enough that it probably makes the current monarchy nervous. How long do you think they will tolerate you—trust you—knowing that you once had enough favor to usurp the throne of their beloved—"

Suddenly I heard my mother's voice in my mind. I could tell by the way Nicias's gaze instantly turned to Darien that he heard her as well.

Perhaps you would *be happiest if you remained in Wyvern's Court,* she said. *If I knew that for certain, I would have insisted that Cjarsa leave you alone. I believe she would have let me have my way; she wants me by her more than she needs you on the island. But it must be your choice. I have been little enough a part of your life as it is. I should not be the one to decide what you do with it now.*

In that moment, it might have been nice if Darien had expressed a bias regarding my decision. It would have been comforting to know she cared, and it would have made choosing easier.

Instead, she turned her attention to Nicias to add, *Even you, Nicias, do not have that right. It is Hai's choice to make.*

And if she says no? Nicias asked.

Let her look on the island with eyes not veiled by Ecl before she decides.

As I did? he challenged again.

My daughter does not have your naïveté, Darien pointed out. *She knows how to use her power perfectly well. No one short of royal blood could use persuasion magics on her without her knowledge, and if they do, you are experienced enough to protect Hai, should you choose to accompany her.*

"Darien, if you are plotting with them, at least let us hear it," Lillian said. "I would like to know why we are being punished if the Lady takes us to task for something you've said."

"Have I spoken a word of treason to you?" Darien asked me and Nicias.

"No," I answered, considering her words.

"That's new," Lillian remarked. "Hai, are you coming with us willingly, or do we need to carry you?"

Nicias grasped my hand. "Araceli told me once that if I returned to the island, it would be as her heir. Is that still the case?"

"Of course," Lillian answered.

"If I understand correctly, that gives me authority over everyone but Cjarsa and Araceli themselves. Including you."

Lillian nodded warily. "We will follow our Empress's commands before yours, but yes, even Cjarsa's Mercy would be held to your will unless she said otherwise."

"Then these are my terms. If Hai goes to Ahnmik, I go with her," he said. "Anyone who tries to use magic to manipulate either of us, or who tries to separate us without

Hai's consent, I will consider to have acted against me—which, according to Ahnmik's laws, gives me every right to execute them. Or at least turn them over to you."

"A'le," Darien answered. "As you wish, *my lord*."

Her tone was so careful, so neutral, it betrayed her pleasure. My mother was concerned with assuring my freedom of choice, but she was not nearly as unbiased when it came to my prince.

CHAPTER 23

I thought about all the times I had seen Nicias on Ahnmik . . .
had seen *myself* there, though I had never imagined that I could
be the woman—the pure-blood falcon—I had often seen by his
side. Now I understood.

"Milady." *The falcon did not kneel to me, but he bowed his
head, his downcast eyes unable to conceal the terror within.* "Please,
forgive a foolish man his ill-conceived words."

*Not incorrect, simply ill-conceived. If Nicias had not been
nearby, his crass comments about* quemak *falcons would never have
elicited any kind of stir.*

"Do you apologize to me," *I asked,* "or to my prince?"

*Ahnmik's magic would not let him lie, no matter how much the
mongrel in question wished it would. The man looked at his prince
and cringed. The* aona'ra *was not in a forgiving mood.*

* * *

Perhaps too late, my mind made the crucial connections between the many *sakkri* I had spun in my life. I knew what would follow if Nicias and I went to Ahnmik now. How many times had I seen it, dreamed it, *wished* I could be that woman beside him?

The royal house would welcome us with open arms. Cjarsa would personally greet me. My mother would watch proudly as I took the trials—and passed, of course. I would be given a rank, and at last I would be able to begin formal study of the *jaes'Ahnmik* magic.

Someone would be able to heal my wings; now that the cobra's taint was gone from me, anyone powerful enough would be able to force-change me and give me back the sky and, with it, everything I had ever wanted. I would dance at the triple arches once again.

And Nicias . . . ah, my prince. He would be beside me. It would bother him at first when people were polite to me only because I had both his favor and Cjarsa's, but I had faced such disdain all my life, and I would convince him to ignore it and let things be.

My mother—my Empress and I would convince this lovely peregrine to accept many things.

I cringed, and though I wanted Nicias's company very much, I said, "You don't have to do this for me."

"I will return to Wyvern's Court after you make your decision, no matter what you do," Nicias replied. "Ahnmik isn't my world and I don't want it. I just don't trust them to let you decide without coercion. If you want to go alone, that is your choice, but I hope you will let me go with you—if only to allow me the comfort of knowing that you are not forced to stay."

What if they try to force you to stay? I asked, keeping the words from the ears and minds of the Empress's Mercy.

Cjarsa's orders to Araceli to let me live my own life aren't likely to have changed, he replied. *And if they have, I doubt your mother will fail to move Ecl and Mehay to get her way—as always.*

As always indeed. But my mother wanted Nicias on the island. *I* wanted Nicias on the island, too, but it was a selfish desire. I could not take him without eventually losing him.

In the end, Nicias was the only master of his fate; he would, or would not, go to the white city of his own volition. All I could hope to do was keep him from destroying himself for me.

If I went, I would miss him. I would miss Wyvern's Court, and even the Obsidian guild. I would regret not seeing Sive Shardae grow into the beautiful queen I knew she would become, and I would miss the cobra king to whom I had so recently offered my allegiance.

"Enough," one of the falcons snapped as I hesitated. "There is no room for negotiation. Hai is one of the Lady's subjects, and so is answerable to the Lady's commands."

"As are we all," Darien answered, and everyone knew exactly what she meant.

Why? Why did I delay?

This world of snakes and birds was filled with such impossible, contrary fools; they struggled daily against the tides of Fate, even when it would be so much wiser to give in.

They burned with an incredible, desperate passion, which perhaps only Anhamirak's followers could truly comprehend. Certainly there was no equivalent among the long-lived *shm'Ahnmik*.

In the white city, there was enough beauty to make the most hardened heart weep. There were music that resonated in the soul and colors that the eye could hardly comprehend.

Pure and crystalline and lovely, Ahnmik was clear of the grime and sweat of Wyvern's Court.

Without intending to, I let out a small sound. Nicias put a hand on my arm, but his eyes stayed on the Mercy, as if he was tying to discover what they had done to me.

"I want to go home," I said softly. "I want to speak to my—" I almost said *mother*, and that was what I meant, but I was not thinking of the mother who was standing before me. "My Empress."

"And if she chooses to see you, then you may," the impatient falcon replied. "Assuming we ever get back to the city."

Darien asked me, "You want to speak to her *now*?"

"The Empress does not grant audiences at the whims of a—"

Darien half lifted her hand and, without even turning, tossed enough magic at her fellow guard to make him stumble to his knees. Closing her eyes, my mother drew a half breath; I could feel her power reaching out with a petition.

To the magic of falcons, distance meant little. The many miles between Wyvern's Court and the island of Ahnmik were bridged by power, until suddenly my heart began to pound and I blinked back tears.

I was still in Wyvern's Court physically, but mentally I stood before my Empress.

"My Lady," I whispered.

"Darien has informed me that I must speak to you." There was some wry amusement in her tone; few people ever "informed" the white Lady of anything, much less told her she must do something.

"My Lady . . . you gave so much to me when I was a child, even though I was born *quemak*. I—"

"You are the only child of my favored companion, Darien," Cjarsa interrupted, her magic wrapping me almost like an embrace, gentle and comforting. "Your father's blood was not your fault. How could I do less than twist Fate herself to give you the chance to come home, whole and pure?"

The words differed a little from what she would have said to my mother, but I recognized the argument I had heard in my recent *sakkri*.

She must have sensed my slight withdrawal, for she continued to make her point.

"It is little enough," she pointed out, "compared to your machinations to save Wyvern's Court."

"My Lady . . ."

I thought about what my mother had told me when we had argued about Oliza. *Cjarsa has more power than you and I combined, but the void frightens her. She fears drowning in its illusions, so she holds back.* My mother's words had frightened me then, but I had not taken the time to understand the full implications of them.

Now Cjarsa had chosen her words carefully, avoiding stating any fact that Ahnmik's magic would reveal to be false.

"You never even looked to the future, did you?" I had nearly drowned trying to save Wyvern's Court. She had let me struggle on my own, and now she tried to take credit for all the incredible twists of Fate and Will that had led to this moment. "You would have seen the dangers of Oliza's reign if you had only *looked,* but you never even tried. You just let me . . ."

"I let you become queen," Cjarsa said.

"You let me tie myself to this realm," I said. "Do you wish me home, my Lady?"

"You are one of us, *shm'Ahnmik'la'Hai.* Your place is here."

Coldness seeped up my spine, as she neglected to answer the question.

"Lady, you know I would do anything you wished. From my earliest memory, you are there, teaching me to dance. You . . ." *You were the one who caught me when I fell and my wings were scoured from me.* "You were everything to me." *You were the one who healed what you could.* "Please, my Empress. *Do you want me to return to you?*"

She hesitated, and in that hesitation I heard the echo of all my last illusions shattering.

You were the one, I thought, *who held me . . . and you were the one who told me to rest. You were the one whose voice carried me into Ecl.*

"All you ever needed to say was that you wanted me," I said. "That day under the arches, if you had only given me a word of encouragement, I would have stayed in this world. I could have used my magic to heal my wings before they set so twisted I would never have them again. I could have . . ." My voice broke. "But instead, you told me to rest. I would be there still if Nicias had not come for me."

I waited, though I knew it was useless. Cjarsa did not continue to argue with me. I loved the white city, but there I was a mongrel, something to be tolerated. Even with "pure" magic, I would never be unblemished. I gathered myself together, drawing in a deep breath rich with the scents of wintertime in Wyvern's Court.

"I may finally be a falcon in your eyes, white Lady, but it is another land that holds my heart. I have no desire to return to Ahnmik. I . . . I have a place here," I said. I wasn't exactly certain what that place was, but over the past few days, I had started to discover a connection to this land that I had never had to Ahnmik.

Oliza did not trust me or like me. I made Sive nervous. The old Diente and Tuuli Thea, Zane and Danica, would probably never forgive me for what I had done to their daughter. And here, too, I would always be an outsider, a mixed-blood falcon.

But here, for a while, I had been needed.

Shaking with fear, I said, "Lady Cjarsa, I respectfully request your permission to stay here, as a citizen of Wyvern's Court and not as one of your subjects."

Such bold words. How could I have said them? How could I, who had been raised by the Lady's hand, even imply that I could be released from her authority?

Brazen, as a cobra cannot help but be. Somewhere in *sakkri*, I had heard Cjarsa say those words, about my father.

Cjarsa sighed, and I struggled not to tremble in the face of her disappointment. "Is this really what you want?" she asked.

"My Lady, if you tell me that you *want* me home, that you *want* me beside you, that I have ever been more to you than a nuisance, then I will fly to your side in an instant. But you won't, because Ahnmik will not let you lie that way.

"I saw the fear in your eyes when I was a child and I began to spin *sakkri* of the Dasi. You do not want me in your empire; you tolerated me for years to try to win back my mother's favor, but you never wanted me. Please, grant me permission to leave now."

Time stretched and seemed to slow as I waited for her reply.

"Permission granted."

I had tears in my eyes as I pulled myself out of the trance and away from the last time I would ever see the woman who had raised me.

I would probably love her all my life, as a child must love her mother. I certainly would not be able to hate her. I understood her fear too well to not forgive her.

"I don't understand," Darien said, standing beside where I knelt with one hand pressed to the soil of Wyvern's Court. "You told her no?"

"You said it would be her decision," Nicias pointed out. "Cjarsa has honored—"

"I never thought she would actually *choose* this!" Darien replied. "Hai, what do you have here? What place does any falcon have in a serpent and avian land?"

"Darien," Nicias said, intervening, "she made her decision."

I pushed myself to my feet, to face my mother. Looking into her Ahnmik silver eyes, I felt as if I was looking at a stranger.

"I have never been a falcon, not in your eyes, or the eyes of Ahnmik, or my Empress's or even my own. I was always . . . tainted. I'm cobra blood, Darien."

"You *used* to be," she asserted. "You know I loved your father, but I hated the curse he left you with. You've rid yourself of that now."

"The curse he left me with was passion," I replied. "And yes, it hurts, but it is *mine*. And the gift he left me with was Wyvern's Court."

"You would really stay here, when Cjarsa has offered you Ahnmik?" My mother looked at me with confusion. "Hai, all your life, I have struggled to give you this—"

"All my life, you have struggled to give *yourself* this," I said. "Struggled to win, against the Empress."

"Haven't you?"

"Darien . . . *Mother* . . . you are *shm'Ahnmik*. And the white god has no patience for right and wrong, or sacrifice, only power."

"You're one of us."

I shook my head. "In the first *sakkri* I ever saw, I watched through Kiesha's eyes as Cjarsa and Araceli ripped Anhamirak's magic in half. I screamed with the cobra, until my throat bled and I lost my voice for weeks. I should have known on that day that I would never be a falcon."

Those around me knew my heritage by my ebony hair. I knew that it was held somewhere even deeper than magic . . . and that it wasn't on the white island. It never had been.

"You will stay in this land, without a serpent form?" Darien asked, in a last desperate plea. "Hai, I do not understand you. You had Wyvern's Court in your hand, and you gave it up. You gave up your cobra form, and your position as Diente. Why else would you have done that, if not to come home?"

"I gave up my magic to save my cousin's *life*," I said. "I am more than my animal form. I am more than the magic the royal house of Ahnmik deemed right for the serpiente to retain. I am more than feathers or scales.

"*I am* Kiesha'ra."

EPILOGUE

Months later, I still sometimes woke in the night, coated in sweat, with my heart pounding. Wrapped in Nicias's arms, I would open my eyes and take a deep breath to assure myself that the past half year had really happened.

As a child, I had centered my entire life on my Empress's desires; I had sought nothing more than to please her, even when she had sent me into Ecl. Now I had cut my ties to Ahnmik and was responsible for myself, for my own decisions, and for my own future. I had lost all guidance beyond myself and had chosen this heartache of decision that made serpents and avians so brilliantly alive: freedom.

Though flavored by tears, that freedom was the sweetest thing I had ever known.

After the weeks of chaos, from Oliza's abdication through Salem's resurrection, Wyvern's Court did not return instantly to rest. Both royal houses came together to try to heal their shaken world, like parents holding a child through her night terrors. There was much shuddering and wailing, but eventually the court returned to its precious balance of two worlds dancing together in defiance of Fate herself.

I was honored to say I was among the dancers.

On this night, I stood in the center of the Obsidians' camp, surrounded by all their guild, as well as some more unusual faces—the exiled falcons from the candle shop, and an uneasy-looking Sive Shardae, who was standing beside her serpiente companion. The only light came from a single lamp hanging on one of the nearest trees, and from the stars high above us.

Vere stood before me, dressed in black, with a silver *melos* about his waist.

"Your people have fared badly in all this," I said to him as we waited for the last guests to arrive. "First Oliza made you promises, and then I did, and now neither of us is in a position to keep them. I am sorry."

A rustling in the forest announced the arrival of three newcomers: Salem; his Naga, Rosalind; and Nicias, who had guided them here. Nicias came to my side and wrapped me in his arms.

Vere nodded a greeting and then continued our conversation. "You really think we have been mistreated by these events?" the white viper asked. "Look around. The cobra king and his mate are peaceful guests in our camp, traveling dancers and—albeit nervous—friends." He gestured at Sive, who was now deep in conversation with Maya. "You say we've come out badly, but look around. You'll see *Maeve'ra, Kiesha'ra, shm'Ahnmik* and the descendant of Alasdair standing together."

"It's an exception," I replied. "Tomorrow—"

"It is an exception that has never before occurred over the

course of thousands of years. And tomorrow, even if the fighting begins again, they will remember." He smiled in a way that said that he knew his words were dangerously optimistic, but that he couldn't help it. "I never wanted to be a king, Hai," he assured me. "I accepted your suit because I felt it was time to reach out and make alliances, but I am pleased with the way things have turned out."

His smile became a little more wistful as his gaze flickered from me to Nicias, but all he said was "Are you ready?"

I drew a long, deep breath, taking in all the scents of the wild forest, and raised my face to the night sky.

"I'm ready."

As I stepped onto the camp's center dais, I allowed myself once more to reach out to my lover and foe. Carefully, I asked Ecl's favor. There was only one thing I needed to know.

It was a strange world, taken over by humanity and stretching farther than anyone had imagined. Vast oceans, unknown continents, machines that did the work of men . . . What an incredible world it had become in the centuries since my own life. And within that world:

Two women stood face to face, garnet eyes looking deeply into gold. The cobra began to laugh, then hugged the hawk joyously. The Tuuli Thea was crying, but they were sweet tears.

Both knelt beside a baby girl with white-blond hair and golden eyes. The next Tuuli Thea's father—a white viper, one of the few remaining children of Obsidian—leaned nearby, watching trustingly as the Diente picked up the hawk-viper child.

None of them knew what their ancestors had gone through—what risks had been taken, or what sacrifices had been made—to allow them to stand there unafraid.

I pulled back from the vision as easily as I breathed, as I heard the drumbeat begin. Mentally, I sent a kiss to the familiar abyss, but the one it sent in return did not restrain me.

My eyes still closed, I lifted myself onto my toes, arching my back and crossing my wrists above my head. I listened to my heart as it began to beat in time with the drummer's rhythm. The flute, when it began to play, felt like an extension of my own breath.

My audience gasped as I unfurled wings the color of a cobra's scales, with a span of more than fifteen feet. Because my magic was finally under control, Nicias and—grudgingly—Oliza had been able to work together to heal them. Now, as I prepared to dance, I spread them wide.

Yes, I had finally embraced my Cobriana heritage, but who said snakes weren't meant to fly?

My prayer is simple, my child, my child,
Please, do try to understand:
I've given you freedom, and left you with
choices.
Now you're at the beginning,
Again.

About the Author

Amelia Atwater-Rhodes grew up in Concord, Massachusetts. Born in 1984, she wrote her first novel, *In the Forests of the Night*, praised as "remarkable" (*Voice of Youth Advocates*) and "mature and polished" (*Booklist*), when she was thirteen. She has since published *Demon in My View, Shattered Mirror,* and *Midnight Predator,* all ALA Quick Picks for Young Adults; *Hawksong,* a *School Library Journal* Best Book of the Year and a *Voice of Youth Advocates* Best Science Fiction, Fantasy, and Horror selection; *Snakecharm; Falcondance;* and *Wolfcry.*